GIRL WITH A GOLD WING

It's the 1960s, and Cora Murray dreams of taking to the skies — so when her father shows her a recruitment advertisement for air hostesses, she jumps at the chance to apply. Passing the interview with flying colours, she throws herself into her training, where she is quite literally swept off her feet by First Officer Ross Anderson. But whilst Ross is charming and flirtatious, he's also engaged — and Cora's former boyfriend Dave is intent on regaining her affections . . .

Books by Jill Barry
in the Linford Romance Library:

DREAMS OF YESTERDAY

JILL BARRY

GIRL WITH A GOLD WING

Complete and Unabridged

LINFORD
Leicester

First published in Great Britain in 2013

First Linford Edition
published 2014

A catalogue record for this book is available
from the British Library.

ISBN 978–1–4448–2223–6

Published by
F. A. Thorpe (Publishing)
Anstey, Leicestershire

Set by Words & Graphics Ltd.
Anstey, Leicestershire
Printed and bound in Great Britain by
T. J. International Ltd., Padstow, Cornwall

This book is printed on acid-free paper

1

Cora perched on the arm of her father's fireside chair and leaned in to see what had caught his attention in the newspaper. He jabbed his finger at the boxed advertisement. She caught her breath. Ever since Cora's mum had taken her to watch a 1950s film about air stewardesses, the urge to take to the skies hadn't faded. Now the words she read in the 'Situations Vacant' column sent tingles down her spine. Could her dream come true?

'What do you think then?' Mr Murray rustled his newspaper.

'It's not the time to job hunt, Dad. Christmas is coming, remember.'

'But you have to agree this is something special. Don't let your mum talk you out of applying. Bless her, she'd like to see you married and living round the corner. Give yourself a chance to follow your dreams.'

Cora's heart beat a little faster, knowing her father was gently guiding her. Giving her that little push she needed.

'*Expanding independent airline based in Glasgow seeks applications for the position of airhostesses for their Bristol base. Applicants should be aged 21–25 years, be of smart appearance and enjoy good health. Training course begins in Gatwick, February 1965.*'

'Well?'

'Of course I'm interested, Dad. I was only waiting for my 21st to arrive.'

'You'll be 21 by the time the course starts. Ring up and ask for an application form.'

'I daren't risk phoning from work. Imagine if anyone caught me! But I'll write a letter tonight. Being based at Bristol would be great.'

Mr Murray tore carefully round the advertisement and handed it to Cora. She gazed at it as if she held an invitation to a Buckingham Palace garden party.

'What's up?' Her mum edged through the door, bringing cups of tea and chocolate digestives.

'Dad's found an airline that's recruiting hostesses for their Bristol base.' Cora watched the corners of her mother's mouth turn down.

'It's only a suggestion,' Roy Murray protested. 'The lass has always had itchy feet.'

'Air hostesses?' Arlene Murray reacted as though Cora was considering a lion-taming job.

'It'll probably come to nothing.' Cora's cheeks reddened. 'They'll be looking for sophisticated girls — girls with far more qualifications than I have.'

'If you're good enough to run Gigi Fashions, you're good enough to serve cups of tea and hand out sick bags. Now, what's on the box at eight?'

Cora's dad winked at her. Her mum offered her a biscuit. Cora hesitated. If by some amazing quirk of fate she gained an interview, she'd feel trimmer if she cut down on sweet things.

'I'd better not,' she said.

★　★　★

The letter she'd been awaiting burnt a hole in Cora's handbag as she walked to work a few days later, but she stowed it in her locker until lunchtime. Once inside her favourite milk bar, she found a corner table and unfolded the application form.

Thanks to a school exchange trip, Cora spoke fairly fluent French and had never minded exams; but when her teachers recommended a secretarial course, she'd meekly accepted. She was still surprised to have reached the lofty heights of assistant manager in a gown shop, having taken a sales job after discovering the command to 'take a letter, Miss Murray' wasn't for her. She read the questions, trying not to let her imagination soar too much.

★　★　★

Two weeks later, Cora stood in the hallway of her home, poised for what she knew must be the most important day of her life so far.

'I wish you weren't doing this. But I must say, you look the part.' Mrs Murray, clothes brush in hand, gave her daughter a final once-over.

'Thanks to my Chanel suit. It doesn't often get an airing.'

'It brought you luck in your last interview. Your hair's gone up nicely too, though I say it myself.' Mrs Murray glanced at her watch. 'Time to go, if you don't want to miss your train.'

Cora kissed her mum's cheek and pulled on a pair of emerald-green suede gloves. 'Thanks for the packed lunch.'

'It should stop your tummy rumbling.'

If the butterflies already stomping around will allow it, thought Cora. Now her interview day had arrived, she still couldn't believe it. Booking a day off had been easy, as everyone assumed she was visiting Bristol for Christmas shopping. If they knew about her appointment with Maggie Martin, chief hostess of Castle Airways, would they, as did her mum, think she was stark-staring crazy? The name Maggie suggested a kind, smiley sort of person. Being rejected surely wouldn't be too bad if Miss Martin proved as friendly as her name suggested?

⋆ ⋆ ⋆

A friendly young woman showed Cora into a small room off the airport concourse. 'Take a seat, Miss Murray,' she said. 'Miss Martin won't keep you long.'

'Thank you,' said Cora. 'I hope I don't look too windblown.' She smoothed her dark hair, worn in a French plait that day.

'You look very smart and not in the least windblown. I do like that navy braiding on the emerald green.'

Feeling a tad braver, Cora took a

deep breath. 'Thank you.' She hesitated.

'Am I . . . Are there many other applicants?'

The young woman's eyes danced. 'Just a few,' she said. 'Miss Martin whittled the list down to 12 out of 100 hopefuls.'

'My goodness!' Cora's tummy lurched.

'So you should feel pleased to get this far.'

'I suppose.' Cora wrinkled her snub nose. 'Interviews always terrify me.'

'Me too. I'm Linda, by the way. I work for the airport but Castle Airways have borrowed me today.' She smiled at Cora. 'Their counter's still being built, as you probably noticed. The airline's operating new routes and it's the first time they've had a Bristol base.'

'I see,' said Cora. 'Do you know what the uniforms look like?'

'Miss Martin's wearing hers today. She reminds me of that model girl — Jean Shrimpton, isn't it? Fashion plate's the expression my mum would use.'

Cora's small balloon of confidence shrank like a soufflé left standing too long. When a vision in blue appeared in the doorway and fixed her with an appraising stare, she understood what Linda meant. Cora rose, forgetting her handbag, which plummeted to the floor. Hastily she retrieved it, but had no chance to apologise for her clumsiness.

'Miss Murray? I'm sorry to keep you waiting. Now, Linda, I'm expecting Glasgow to call back; but if I'm still interviewing, please tell them I'll ring as soon as I'm free.'

'Of course.' Linda closed the door behind her.

The chief air hostess walked towards the table. Maggie Martin might have been poured into her slate-blue pencil skirt and fitted jacket. Upon one lapel gleamed a gold half-wing. Sheer nylons and navy blue court shoes completed the elegant effect.

'Please sit down, Miss Murray. May I call you Cora?'

8

'Of course.' Cora placed her handbag on the floor so it could fall no further and sat back, trying to look relaxed.

'You were born in Scotland, I see.' Maggie scanned Cora's application. 'We have no vacancies at Glasgow Airport. I hope you realise that.'

'I do,' said Cora. 'My father was based in Scotland when I came along. He was in the RAF. Since they posted him south, we've lived about thirty miles from Bristol.'

Not a flicker of a smile. Not a whisper of interest as to whether Mr Murray had been a pilot or not. Maggie Martin pushed a card across the table. 'Could you read that aloud, please?'

Cora stopped admiring the older woman's glossy peach nail polish and focused on the print. At first the words danced before her eyes, but she took a deep breath and read aloud a safety instruction, taking care not to rush.

'Thank you,' said Maggie. 'Are you able to relay that same information in French?'

Cora did so, thanking her lucky stars she remembered how to translate 'fasten your seatbelts please'.

'Good. Now, would you mind standing and walking to the window?'

Cora rose, smoothing down her skirt. When she reached the window, she turned and stood, arms at her sides, trying not to feel fazed by Miss Martin's cold, appraising stare.

'You're not 21 until January.'

'I didn't want to miss this chance,' said Cora, watching the ghost of a smile tug the chief hostess's lips.

'Have you ever done any modelling?' Maggie tapped an almond-shaped fingernail against her front teeth and consulted her paperwork. 'You move gracefully.'

Cora brightened. 'I've done a bit at the store. Part of my role is arranging fashion shows and introducing new ranges for the season.'

'Do you enjoy the work?'

Cora sensed a trick question. If she enthused about her job, Miss Martin would surely question her motivation. If she said she disliked it, she might appear desperate to find something — anything — to help her escape.

'I enjoy talking to people and I get on well with my colleagues,' she said. 'But I think it's time to move on.'

'Someone spotted your potential. Most young women would be encouraged to stay and take the next step.'

'I agree, but there's something about aviation that fascinates me.'

Maggie pounced. 'Don't imagine this job's glamorous. Sometimes you'll be up at the crack of dawn. Sometimes you'll still be on your feet at midnight. Some passengers are so frightened of flying they snap at the cabin crew. You must never answer back.'

'I'm used to dealing with customer complaints.'

'Have you ever travelled by air?'

'Once to Paris — and home again, of course.' Cora chuckled but the older woman didn't crack a smile.

'I see you've no nursing experience.'

Cora didn't comment. Everyone knew airlines liked employing former nurses as stewardesses.

'But you possess a first-aid certificate. That's something. What would you do if a passenger went into premature labour while you were airborne?'

★ ★ ★

'Flippin' heck. What did you say when she asked you that? Pass the bread and butter, dear.'

Arlene Murray moved the china plate with the butterflies on closer to her husband. 'Give the girl a chance to eat her tea, Roy. It sounds like she's had a hard time.'

Cora waved her fork and swallowed. 'It was like trying to dodge a deadly snake.'

Her mum raised her eyebrows. 'You say she's an attractive, elegant woman? Maybe she's been disappointed in love.'

'Not every woman yearns for wedding bells, Mum. I'm not exaggerating when I say Miss Martin's like a model. But she turned me into a twelve-year-old, back in my gymslip, getting a wigging for forgetting my gym shoes.'

'Do you think she was the same with everybody?'

'The girl helping her said two of the morning candidates dived straight for the ladies' after their interviews.'

Arlene pursed her lips. 'Strikes me, you'd be better staying at Gigi's where you're appreciated. When that nice manager of yours finishes work, you're sure to get her job.'

Cora's manager, Em, expected a baby in the spring and had dropped hints of likely promotion. This knowledge, although appreciated, couldn't fix Cora's restlessness.

'Wait and see,' said Roy. 'If the airline offers you a place, that's the time you make your decision.'

'What if she goes but doesn't like it? She'll have burnt her bridges with Gigi and it'll be back to the 'Situations

Vacant'.' Arlene stabbed her fork into a roast potato.

'Mum, I think it's unlikely I've impressed Miss Martin. She said she'd be in touch soon, whatever the verdict. Dad's right. It's pointless worrying about something until it happens.'

'You certainly don't get your travel bug from me.' Her mum shuddered. 'Beats me how your dad became so keen on aeroplanes.'

'Didn't I spend half the war years on an RAF base?' He winked at Cora. 'Tell you what, whether or not you get this job, it's high time your mum and I went on one of those package holidays.'

'That's a great idea.' Cora noticed Arlene's expression and chuckled. 'Don't worry, Mum. If you fly with Castle, I imagine Miss Martin's far too important to be working on your flight.'

* * *

When Cora left for work the following Monday, Castle still hadn't contacted

14

her. Perhaps the two successful applicants had already been informed and
Miss Martin wanted to be sure they
accepted before breaking the hearts of
the unfortunate ten. Cora pulled her
scarf more snugly around her throat.
The sky's sullen look signalled snow
and she wished she'd heeded her
father's warning. He didn't appreciate
how the other girls would giggle if their
assistant manageress turned up wearing
wellies.

Inwardly she groaned, seeing the
young man crossing the road towards
her. Dave, her former boyfriend, had
got fed up when she'd insisted on
enrolling for two courses at night
school. He'd stormed off and found
consolation elsewhere; but since his
engagement had ended recently, he'd
lost no opportunity to cry on her
shoulder. She didn't like to snub him
but the situation was fast becoming
uncomfortable.

'Good morning, gorgeous,' he called.
'Are you talking to me?'

'Who else? Cora, how do you fancy coming to the pictures tonight?' He fell into step.

'Sorry, Dave. I meet with my manager after work on a Monday, so I'll be late home.'

'Why not stay in town? We could grab a quick snack, then go on to the Plaza. They're showing *Wonderful Life*. All you girls like Cliff Richard, don't you?'

Cora glanced up at a sulky sky. 'It might snow, Dave. It's nice of you to ask, but . . . '

'I shan't give up, Cora. Heaven knows I'm sorry I ended our relationship, but you must know I'd never have gone out with Sue in the first place if you hadn't played silly games.'

Cora stopped and glared at him. 'You were the one who got the huff because I wasn't prepared to spend every single night of the week in your company.'

They walked on in silence until he began whistling the title song from *Wonderful Life*. Out of tune. Seething,

16

she almost stepped beneath a workman's ladder propped against the sturdy brick facade of Floyd's Bank. Dave clutched her arm and she let him steer her along the pavement edge. Didn't she need every possible crumb of luck?

'Look,' she said. 'I've got a lot on my mind but if you like, maybe closer to Christmas, we could go for a drink or a meal.'

They were nearing the shop. Dave released her arm. 'I suppose that's better than nothing. Don't leave it too long though, Cora. I miss you, I really do.' He leaned in and kissed her cheek.

'Have a good day.' She hurried to the door, hoping Em had arrived so she wouldn't have to fumble for her key. Cora darted inside, leaving Dave heading for the town council offices where he worked.

Cora crossed the deserted ground floor to the staff room, unbuttoning her coat on the way. Em called out to her.

'Good morning, Cora. When you're

ready, could you check those shift dresses — the ones with the fluted sleeves? I think the black's sold out.'

'How about removing the one in the window display? We could dress the dummy in scarlet. Maybe add some gold jewellery? It is the party season, after all.'

'That's a good idea. We have two salesgirls off today, don't forget.'

'We probably won't be rushed off our feet but I'll keep an eye on both floors.'

Cora hurried off. She didn't even think of her recent interview, especially as her prophesy had proved wrong. Throughout the day, several regular customers braved the December chill to choose a special Christmas frock. Wool jersey dresses in emerald, royal blue and scarlet flew off the racks while little black numbers sparkling with sequins were snapped up so swiftly, Cora had to ring the Bristol branch to request a special delivery.

At close of business, Em came through from the office wearing her coat and hat. 'I'm sorry, Cora, but my head's thumping. We'll have to have our weekly meeting tomorrow. Thanks for all your hard work today.'

'I've enjoyed it. You make sure you put your feet up. Tell that husband of yours it's cold meat and pickles night and he's doing the honours.'

Em smiled. 'OK. I'll leave you to lock up, then.'

When Cora left, she glanced in both directions to make sure Dave wasn't around before setting off. If she bumped into him, he'd be sure to think she'd made up the whole Monday meetings thing.

She suddenly visualised Maggie Martin. How would it feel to hold down a top job like hers? She decided if Castle Airways turned her down, she wouldn't give up on her dream. There were plenty of other airlines, and her 21st birthday wasn't far away.

2

The silver salver on the hall table contained a slim white envelope. Cora eyed it, wiping her feet on the coconut matting inside the door. Her tummy lurched when she noted the first class stamp and her name heading the neatly typed address.

'You're early for a Monday, love.' Her mum appeared in the living room doorway. 'Was it snowing in town? We had a few flakes but nothing much.' She watched Cora pick up her letter. 'Oh yes. Postie was late. One of the vans broke down.' She turned and went back to the gently murmuring television.

Cora had expected to see a Glasgow postmark, but of course the newspaper advert had mentioned Gatwick for training. She felt her heart attempt a somersault as she ripped open the envelope.

Dear Miss Murray,

Air Hostess Vacancy
at Bristol Airport

Thank you for attending for an interview on 9ᵗʰ December. I am pleased to inform you that you have been successful in obtaining a place on the training course commencing Monday 15th February 1965 at Gatwick Airport. Your accommodation will be arranged for the duration of the course.

Cora skimmed the rest, struggling to focus on starting salary, uniform provision and everything she needed to know, but still her gaze kept devouring that thrilling second sentence.

In a daze she shrugged off her coat and pulled off her black patent court shoes before padding upstairs in stockinged feet. If her mum wasn't focused on her favourite TV show, she'd surely be questioning the letter's contents.

Cora, hugging the news to herself, realised that having been offered this chance, she was far hungrier for it than anyone would ever know, except maybe her dad.

She wriggled out of her dark grey dress and cream satin slip and reached inside her wardrobe for black slacks and a fluffy pink jumper. Before rummaging under the bed for her slippers, Cora picked up the letter to read again, just as she heard the front door bang. It stuck a bit these days and needed a good shove. Her father kept meaning to fix it, which considering his skill at mending aeroplane engines, always made her smile. He'd be delighted with her news.

She ran downstairs in time to help her mother dish up the meal, hugging her secret to herself until the family sat around the kitchen table.

'Aren't you longing to know what my letter said, Mum?'

'I clean forgot! Was it from that airline? Don't take it to heart, love.

Some things aren't meant to be.'

'What's all this?' Her dad frowned.

'Castle Airways have offered me a place on the training course.'

He dropped his cutlery with a clatter. 'That's marvellous news!'

Her mum's mind had clearly been fast-forwarding to her evening's viewing. 'What's so marvellous that you've spilt gravy on the tablecloth, dear?'

'Our lass is taking to the skies, Arlene. I can't wait to tell the blokes at work.'

Arlene stared at her daughter. 'You got the job? You're going to become one of those air hostesses?'

'If all goes well.' Cora smiled at her mum's horrified expression. 'I still can't believe Miss Martin liked me enough to offer me a place.'

'I thought she wouldn't let you slip through the net,' said Roy Murray. 'Do you know how many others she chose?'

'I'm not sure but they only need two girls at Bristol.'

'What I don't understand, Cora, is

why you haven't shown any interest in applying to airlines before now. It's a bit spur-of-the-moment for me.' Arlene's tone rang as frosty as the wintry windowpanes.

'Mum, I didn't want to trouble you over something that might have remained a dream.'

Her mother still looked puzzled. 'How have I not noticed your head was in the clouds?'

'You were nursing Nana after her operation and I thought you had enough on your plate without listening to my starry ideas. I didn't start applying to airlines, because you have to be at least 21 before you're allowed to fly. Dad saw that advert and you know the rest.'

'Well, I always knew you were a thoughtful girl,' said Arlene. 'Good with people too.' She pulled a pristine white hanky from her apron pocket and pressed it to her lips.

'Come on, dear,' said Roy Murray soothingly. 'Our Cora's not flying to the moon, you know.

Cora blinked away a tear. 'I don't think even Castle Airways are licensed to land there, Dad.'

'It'll be a performance, trying to get to the airport and back again at night,' said Arlene. 'How will you manage?'

'There's plenty of time to help the lass find somewhere to live in Bristol.'

Cora smiled gratefully at her dad. She knew her mum hadn't expected this and quite honestly, nor had she. Sleep would be elusive that night, but how she relished her bubble of happiness.

★　★　★

Em's little bump wasn't quite so little now and she wore a charcoal-grey maternity dress with a floppy white bow at its neck. Cora had decided to write her letter of resignation during the Christmas break, so Em could discuss the situation with Gigi's managing director afterwards.

But on the Saturday evening, as Cora

handed over the takings, Em surprised her.

'There's something I have to say to you, Cora. My husband wants me to hand in my notice because he's afraid I'll get too tired if I go on working. You know what this means? I'm recommending you take over my job.'

'Em, I . . . I don't know what to say.'

'I know I planned to stay until late March, but I can't say I'm sorry to leave. It's a wonderful opportunity for you, Cora. You can handle the responsibility and your pay will increase of course. What do you say to that?'

★   ★   ★

When Cora left the store, she paused to admire the eye-catching window display. A group of mannequins wearing party frocks and glittering jewellery stood among heaped gold and silver crackers and shiny gift boxes. But thinking how disappointed Em had been, she went on her way, hardly noticing the snowflakes dancing in the air.

'I never dreamt you'd go and do something like that!' Em's surprised words had hit Cora hard. The manageress had changed her tune and hastily congratulated her, but Cora knew this bombshell meant Em's husband would have to be patient a little longer before he had his wife at home full-time.

She'd accepted Dave's invitation to go for a meal that evening. He'd insisted on calling for her and of course, arrived early. With her bedroom door open while she fixed her lipstick and backcombed her dark hair, Cora heard Arlene ask about his Christmas plans.

'You look lovely,' he said, watching her descend, dressed in a Mary Quant blue mini-dress and knee-high black boots.

'Thanks,' she said. 'I hope I won't be poor company. Work's been hectic.'

'You could never be anything but

delightful company.' He kept gazing at her.

She grabbed her coat and Dave scrambled to help her into it, while Arlene looked on approvingly.

'I'm driving Dad's Ford,' he said. 'I thought we'd take a run out to that inn at Edlington. They always keep a log fire burning.'

'He's spoiling you,' said Arlene fondly.

'I'm looking forward to a nice, friendly evening,' said Cora, determined Dave shouldn't think she was letting down her defences.

He held her elbow protectively as they walked to his car. During the journey he chatted about the football team he supported, and soon they pulled into the inn's car park.

'The snow's held off and people are getting in the mood for Christmas,' said Dave. 'Good job I reserved a table.'

'You'll make someone a very happy woman one day.' Cora reached for the door handle.

In moments he was out of the car and beside her. 'I didn't intend saying anything yet, but do I have any chance at all, Cora? I promise not to push my luck but you must know how ashamed of myself I am. I treated you appallingly.'

They picked their way towards the entrance. 'Hang on to me,' he said.

She was glad of his arm. The cold air stung her cheeks, but the windows glowed invitingly and a happy buzz of chatter drifted on the air when a couple of people emerged. The man held open the door, calling, 'Merry Christmas.'

Inside, Dave said, 'Let's have a drink first. Please don't answer my question yet. All I ask is you give it serious thought.'

Seated at a corner table for two with a crackling log fire scenting the air, Cora watched Dave perform the ritual of sniffing and sipping the wine.

'Cheers. Here's to a merry Christmas and a happy New Year. And to us.' He raised his glass to her.

She took a sip of chilled German hock, then put down her glass as menus arrived. She mustn't let Dave imagine they could turn back the clock and she needed to make her position clear.

After they'd ordered, he sat back, smiling. 'I never brought you here in the old days. Life's different now I can drive.'

'Dave, I have some news. You have to understand that what I'm about to say comes as a result of much thought on my part. It's not a snap decision.' She poured out her story. He listened in silence. Plates of succulent steak and crisp chips arrived but fortunately neither of them appeared to lack an appetite. When she told Dave she'd be off to Gatwick in mid-February, she saw his hand tremble as he refilled her glass.

'I'd better tell you your mother invited me to call round on Christmas afternoon.'

'You know you're welcome. I don't see why we can't stay friends.'

'Just good friends, eh? Do I mean nothing more than that?' His lips set in a thin line.

'I'm too independent for you.'

'That's one of your best qualities. I'd never try to change your mind about flying. I'm pleased for you, I really am.'

'It's the chance of a lifetime,' said Cora.

'I'm just imagining going into work and telling everyone my girlfriend's an airhostess. We'd make the perfect team — you flying and me in a steady job, always there when you need me. I suppose you'll have to find digs in Bristol? You might be lonely. Don't shut me out, please.' He sounded sincere and he made a good point. She didn't want to hurt him but the more he begged, the less she wanted to listen.

'It hurt when you finished with me, Dave.' She buttered the last fragment of bread roll.

'For that, I can only apologise. I was head over heels in love with you, Cora. I acted hastily and I got what I deserved

31

when Sue found someone else. She probably realised I still carried a torch for you.'

His pleading brown eyes only increased Cora's resolve. 'I'm sorry but it'd never work,' she said gently. 'If you want to take someone else out, you should.'

'It's up to me to win you back. We're both different people now and I'm aware your life will change once you leave Pennington. Maybe you're hoping some handsome pilot will sweep you off your feet?' He sounded bitter. 'Isn't that what's supposed to happen?'

Cora laughed. 'Have you been borrowing your mum's romance novels? I expect some pilots marry hostesses just as some teachers marry other teachers.' She pushed aside her plate and leaned towards him. 'I'm hardly likely to throw myself at an airline pilot knowing full well I'd have to resign my job when I married.'

Dave smirked. 'Let's hope their loss is my gain.'

'You're incorrigible,' said Cora. 'But, seriously, having got this far, I'm determined to get through training so I don't have to come back home with my tail between my legs.'

'Fair enough,' he said. 'Now, how about a dessert? Is that allowed for a future air hostess?'

'I'll worry about my figure once Christmas is over.'

★   ★   ★

'It was awful, Dad. Em looked stricken when I finally managed to tell her.'

Father and daughter were washing up together next evening, Arlene having scurried out to attend a rehearsal of the local WI choir.

'You mustn't feel guilty. That firm's been good to you but you've more than earned your wages.'

'Em's thrilled for me but it means she may not be able to leave as soon as she hoped.'

'And you've handed in your notice

33

earlier than planned?'

'I've put it in writing now, instead of waiting until after Christmas,' said Cora. 'Em knows I'd like to take any holiday I'm owed before I start training.'

Her dad picked up a saucepan and began wiping it. 'You know what your mum will say?'

Cora's grin was wry. 'Something along the lines of not looking a gift horse in the mouth? Swiftly followed by a reminder of what a good catch Dave is.'

'She means well but you're chalk and cheese, the pair of you. She doesn't understand why you don't stick with your job and team up with the lad again.'

Cora untied her apron. 'Do you think I'm doing the right thing, Dad?'

'Throwing away a probable promotion? Starting from square one? Yes, I do. I think you'll love flying, and I also think if you back down and tell Miss Martin you've changed your mind, you'll spend the rest of your life regretting it.'

★ ★ ★

After Cora handed in her notice, the Christmas rush merged into the January sales. Mary Quant designs flew off the racks and the company allocated zigzag striped skirts with matching long socks for their sales assistants to wear. Cora admired their striking outfits but dreamed of the smart blue uniform to which she aspired.

Em treated her to lunch on her last day. They toasted one another with orange juice and Cora made Em promise to let her know when the baby arrived.

'I sometimes feel like pinching myself to check whether or not I'm dreaming,' said Cora while they tucked into Welsh rarebit.

'Whereas I have a permanent reminder to tell me I'm not.' Em discreetly patted her bump.

3

Cora had marked three advertisements for accommodation to let in Bristol. She needed to rent somewhere from mid-March and had in mind the Clifton area, but the first flat she viewed, although near the suspension bridge, was a basement one and much too big. The second, perched at the top of a faded yet elegant house overlooking the downs, would limit her diet to baked beans on toast. When she viewed the third, its dilapidated condition horrified her.

Heading down Whiteladies Road to find a coffee bar, her eye was caught by a door sign. At the top of a dingy staircase, she found a small reception office.

'May I help?' A receptionist greeted her as she entered the accommodation agency.

'I hope so.' Swiftly, Cora explained her situation.

'March . . . hmm.' The receptionist riffled through a file. 'We're taking bookings on some refurbished bed-sitting rooms in a house near the downs. I can't show you today but I can assure you they'll be immaculate. Each has its own kitchenette plus washbasin for £6 per week.'

'Bathroom and toilet?'

'You'd share one with another person.'

'That shouldn't be a problem. My hours certainly won't be nine to five.'

The receptionist uncapped her pen. 'We're not advertising these yet but I'll take your details if you're interested.'

'I have to go away on a training course. Is there really no chance of a quick look?'

'You seem like the kind of tenant we're seeking for our client so, yes, I'll take you there now. It's only a few minutes' walk.'

★　★　★

'You've agreed to rent something that's still not finished? Is that wise?' Arlene raised her eyebrows at her daughter.

'I'm going back on Friday afternoon when it should be almost ready. Obviously they won't let people move in while the builders are still working, so my tenancy begins just as the course ends. Why don't you come and see it with me, Mum?'

Arlene's face lit up. 'I'd like that. We could make a list of the things you'll need and do some shopping.'

'The bedding's provided and the kitchen utensils, cutlery and crockery.'

Cora's dad nodded. 'Even though the room comes fully fitted, there'll be things needed to make it more home-like. Not that you'll be there much, I reckon.'

'On standby days I'll have to be around in case they ring and call me to the airport. A radio of my own would be super, but I could always take the one from my bedroom.'

'If you come home for a night now

and then, you won't want to carry a wireless around. Your dad and I were wondering about a little gift, so how about you choose a set?'

'Why don't we all go to Bristol? I could finish work early for once,' said Roy. 'If you haven't found that vanity case you're after for overnight stops, we can try that big store you and your mother like.'

Cora got up and jigged around the kitchen. 'It's so exciting! Thanks, Dad. Thanks, Mum.' She hugged each in turn. 'Just think, if I work hard and pass the exams, I'll become Air Hostess Murray. Oh, I can't wait!'

'Don't go forgetting your final vaccination,' warned her mother, pointing to the calendar. 'Though why you need to be injected against catching yellow fever and malaria, I'll never know. Not canoeing up the Yangtze River, are you?'

Cora caught her father's eye and they both laughed.

'What have I said?'

'Nothing, dear. It's just that our girl will be mixing with all kinds of people, some of whom will have been to exotic places. Better safe than sorry.'

* * *

Before ringing the doorbell, Cora stood outside the front door of her temporary lodgings, watching the lights of her taxi disappear down the road.

'You must be Miss Baker or Miss Murray?' A smiling grey-haired woman dressed in crimson jumper and grey slacks answered the door. She grabbed Cora's case. 'Come in anyway.'

'Mrs Davies? I'm Cora Murray.' She stepped inside and looked around. The smell of lavender polish hung in the air. 'What a lovely house you have.'

'Thank you. I hope you'll enjoy your stay. Your roommate should be here soon. Are you happy to eat with my family?'

'That sounds good.' Cora, already relaxing, followed her hostess, whose teenage son picked up her case as if it weighed ounces not pounds.

Her room contained twin beds with pale gold eiderdowns. There were brown and white curtains, a squiggly brown and fawn carpet, and buttercup-yellow towels hanging beside the washbasin. 'I'm lucky to have such cosy surroundings to escape to every evening,' said Cora.

'You'll enjoy the course,' said her hostess. 'All my girls bar one have passed with flying colours.'

'Ooh,' said Cora. 'I hope I don't follow in her footsteps.'

'Poor soul got so airsick on a training flight, she decided to go home and apply to the police force.'

The doorbell interrupted. 'That'll be Miss Baker. Supper will be in half an hour, if you want to unpack. Your bathroom's the next door along.'

Cora flipped open her suitcase and wondered what Wendy Baker would be like. She didn't have long to wait.

★　★　★

'I'm glad the airport's within walking distance,' said Wendy as they set off next morning. 'I almost took the wrong tube train yesterday. Don't tell Miss Martin.'

Cora had soon discovered her roommate's infectious gurgle of laughter. 'I won't breathe a word. It'd be awful if she thought her Bristol hostesses had no sense of direction.'

'I still can't believe I'm here,' said Wendy. 'I'm convinced Miss Martin confused me with someone else. She'll probably shriek with horror when I walk in.'

'Same here,' said Cora. 'There's the control tower in the distance so we must be heading the right way.'

'Report straight to the Beehive, the letter said, didn't it?'

'Yes, not the airport itself.'

Wendy's copper curls bounced as they hurried across the road. 'I bet I do something daft, first day!'

'I dropped my handbag at the interview. What's the betting Miss

Martin wondered how I'd manage to carry a tray?'

'But we've got this far. If we do all right, we'll both be based at Bristol. Will you live at home, Cora?'

'It's too far to travel without a car so I'm renting a bedsit.'

'Our house is only a few miles from the airport so I'll save on rent. I'll pay my mother for my keep, of course.'

Cora's tummy lurched. 'So this is the Beehive. Here we go!'

'Good luck, Cora. I'm so pleased to have you as a roommate.'

'Same here, Wendy. Look, there's a notice.'

Wendy read aloud: 'Castle Airways Hostess Training — Room 12.'

They set off along the corridor, peering at numbers. The door they wanted stood open and they were met by the sight of Maggie Martin seated at a table, a bulky manual open before her. A subtle mix of carnations and cinnamon hung in the air.

'Come in,' called Maggie, looking up. 'You're the first to arrive.'

Wendy turned her head as if making sure Cora hadn't changed her mind and escaped. Cora hitched her bag higher on her shoulder and gasped as a young man wearing a tweed sports jacket and grey trousers hurtled past, or would have done had he not collided with the chunky obstacle swinging into his path.

'Chocks away,' he yelled, cannoning into Cora.

They stood, arms around each other, struggling to remain upright. Cora didn't know whether to laugh or cry.

'Crikey,' said Wendy. 'It's like *Brief Encounter*.'

Maggie Martin got to her elegantly-shod feet and stalked forward. 'First Officer Anderson,' she said. 'What do you mean by sabotaging one of my new hostesses?'

The young man flashed her a heartbreaker of a smile. With a sigh, he removed his arms from around Cora and smoothed down his unruly corn-gold hair. 'I can't apologise enough, Miss Martin,' he said. 'Are you all right?' He peered anxiously at Cora.

'Yes, I'm fine thank you. But it was my fault.'

'I shouldn't have been in such a tearing hurry. It was utterly and absolutely my fault.' He still stared at Cora, whose cheeks reddened while several anxious-looking girls approached the group.

Maggie cleared her throat. 'Don't you have somewhere else to be, Ross?'

'Ah, yes, indeed. I'm due a simulator session with Bing Crosby. Mustn't keep him waiting. Goodbye ladies.'

Maggie noticed the puzzled expressions on her trainees' faces. 'He means Captain James Crosby, known for obvious reasons as Bing.' She glanced up at the clock. 'Hang your coats on the hooks at the back, then take your seats please, girls. Six tables with two to each. Thanks for being punctual. Let's hope the others haven't been attacked by Apaches on the London under-ground.'

Maggie's chilly tone would freeze an Eskimo but a pair of blue, blue eyes still danced before Cora's vision. First Officer Anderson had knocked her off her feet in more ways than one.

A pretty girl with short black hair cut in the latest geometric style walked into the room and made to close the door.

'Leave it open please, Felicity. If the others fail to remember the room number, it's to be hoped they'll recognise me.' The chief hostess stood beside her table, arms folded across her chest.

'How does she stop her skirt from creasing?' Wendy whispered to Cora as more young women took their places.

'Something to share with us, Miss Baker?'

'Um, sorry Miss Martin. I was wondering if you'd be giving us tips on how to look immaculate in our uniform.'

'You have a long way to go yet,

Wendy. But I note your interest.'

The last four trainees arrived in a breathless rush. They paused on the threshold and Cora felt a wave of sympathy for them, knowing they were practically gibbering with terror at the thought of keeping the chief air hostess waiting.

'I'm very sorry, Miss Martin,' said one. 'Apparently someone moved your signboard so the arrow pointed the wrong way. We, um, we walked for what seemed like miles, then barged into the simulator room by mistake.'

Maggie's lips almost twitched. 'I hope you enjoyed the experience. Take your places, you four, please.'

Cora wondered what Bing Crosby and Ross Anderson had made of the trainee hostess invasion. Pushing away all thoughts of the blue-eyed young pilot, she concentrated on Maggie Martin.

'First of all we'll find out a little about each other. I'll get the ball rolling.' Cora became conscious of everyone sitting up straight. 'I was born in Dunbartonshire. My father worked in Glasgow and he was posted to Wales just in time to turn me into an angry, resentful teenager. I hated changing schools and eventually escaped to London to work as a shorthand typist. One evening I glanced at someone else's paper and saw Castle Airways were advertising for air hostesses. The rest, as they say, is history.' She sat down. 'Now, who's next?'

Uncertainty rippled through the girls. Maggie smiled. 'Come on! Why don't we begin with you . . . Wendy Baker?'

Wendy, smart in a green accordion-pleated skirt and a black polo-neck jumper, rose from her seat. 'I've lived in Bristol all my life. I like singing and amateur dramatics and couldn't wait to leave school and apply to be a Butlin Redcoat. I worked a season at Ayr before coming home and starting work as a dental receptionist.' She grinned. 'I've always liked the idea of becoming an air hostess and Castle was the first airline to offer me an interview.'

Everyone clapped, Cora loudest of all. How brave was that!

'Cora Murray?'

'Like Miss Martin, I was born in Scotland. We moved to Bristol because of my father's job. I discovered I was hopeless at being someone's secretary so went into fashion retailing and worked my way up. When Castle offered this chance, I knew it was the right thing for me.' She turned her head to look at Maggie. 'I had a list of other airlines ready to approach, when I answered your advertisement.'

'Thank you. We've had the two West Country girls, so now let's travel north. Shirley Plumstead and Cathy McNab will be based at Newcastle Airport.'

Everyone's mini-story was heard. There were two nurses amongst the trainees plus a girl who'd worked in a travel agency and someone who'd been a lab technician. At last, Maggie announced a break. 'Each pair will take turns to serve morning coffee and afternoon tea,' she said. 'Felicity and partner, the urn's ready, and milk's in the jug. Tiffin trays are in place. Two biscuits for everyone, but remember we need to watch our figures, girls, so goodies are strictly off the menu after today.'

'How can she do this to us?' Wendy's anguished mutter made Cora laugh.

The coffee makers were instructed to deliver trays to everyone. 'Not one by one,' protested Maggie. 'You need to balance two or three together, like this.' She made it look easy. 'Remember, this airline isn't equipped with modern aeroplanes and we can't compete with shorter flying times and luxury décor. But we pride ourselves on our time-keeping and our friendly cabin staff.' She looked around. 'On which note, why are you, the air hostess, aboard the aircraft?'

No one spoke.

'Any idea, Felicity?'

'To help the passengers?'

'That's part of your role. Most

importantly, you're there in case of emergency. Over the next weeks, you'll learn everything from where to find fire extinguishers to how to leave the cabin via an emergency chute.' She kept a straight face. 'You'll be given due warning of this drill because you might find it advisable to wear slacks that morning.' She returned to her seat. 'Please remember safety is of paramount importance. You'll learn all the practicalities. The rest is up to you.' Her gaze travelled over her audience. 'Never, ever run in public. People tend to notice uniformed flight crew so always remember you're on show and behave accordingly. I don't ever want to hear of any of my girls being seen drinking alcohol when in uniform.'

Cora shuddered, imagining the possible consequences. She jumped at the sound of her name. 'Cora, come and help hand out these hostess manuals, please. There's a lot of learning to do so you should take them home with you later. But bring them in every day, unless I say otherwise.'

She pointed to two girls who'd dared to exchange whispered remarks whilst she was speaking. 'Everything said within these sessions should be relevant to your training. What do you have to say, Shirley?'

Cora, approaching Shirley's table, saw her cheeks turn bright red and grimaced in sympathy. 'I wondered whether Cathy and I should collect the empties, Miss Martin,' she said. 'I'm sorry I interrupted.'

'No, Shirley, it is I who should apologise. I like your initiative. Yes please, you two can collect the empties and stack them at the back. Then if you'll all turn to your indexes, we'll study aircraft interiors.'

* * *

The trainees headed for the cafeteria after Maggie dismissed them at one o'clock. Cora fell into step with Felicity, the girl with the sharp haircut. 'So, what do you think so far? I'm Cora, by the way.'

'Yes, I remember. I'm plucking up courage to ask Miss Martin to call me by my nickname. It's Fliss. Felicity's rather a mouthful, don't you think?' She chuckled. 'Especially when I'm saddled with Fenton-Grey as a surname.'

'When Miss Martin calls you Felicity, do you feel as though you're back in school?'

'Absolutely,' said Fliss. 'Mummy and Daddy only call me Felicity when I'm in disgrace.'

Cora had already decided Fliss spoke like a BBC news announcer. She wore a pale blue cashmere twin set and pearls teamed with a skirt that screamed haute couture. Fliss fitted the debutante mould and Cora wondered why she wasn't engaged to a nice young man with prospects.

'I noticed a few of the girls exchanging glances when I told everyone I'd worked for a publishing house,' said Fliss. 'I didn't dare say anything about Daddy being a distant relative of the Queen. Please don't tell anyone!'

'I'd love to hear about that some time but you really shouldn't be embarrassed, Fliss. All that's part of our heritage.'

They joined the end of the long queue snaking towards the counter. 'I want to mix with real people, Cora. I'm not afraid of getting my hands dirty and I'm used to people barking orders. Daddy was a brigadier in the army. He may be retired, but he still thinks he's commanding a crack regiment.'

Cora picked up two trays and handed one to Fliss. 'What does he think of your new job?'

'He was somewhat disgruntled to find his *Daily Telegraph* folded at the 'Situations Vacant' pages, especially as I'd ringed the Castle Airways advertisement.'

'Oh dear,' said Cora. 'How did you win him round?'

'To give him his due, he said if I

passed muster, I deserved the job. When the information arrived about those inoculations for horrid diseases, he was delighted. It reminded him of his younger days when he was stationed in Timbuktu or some other far-flung place.'

'Like Cardiff or Benbecula?' The amused voice belonged to a young man joining the queue behind the girls.

4

Cora tried to appear calm. 'First Officer Anderson,' she said. 'We meet again.'

'I'm sorry,' he said. 'But I don't think Miss Martin mentioned your name when we collided in the corridor.'

'I'm Cora Murray. This is Felicity — I mean Fliss . . . um . . .'

'Fliss Fenton-Grey.' She held out her right hand.

Ross shook it solemnly, then shook hands with Cora. 'Are you both going to be based at Gatwick?'

'I am,' said Fliss. 'I'm escaping leafy Kew and hoping to find a house share locally.'

'I'm to be based at Bristol,' said Cora. Her heart double-jumped as she detected the tiniest flicker of interest in the first officer's forget-me-not blue eyes.

'So you're imprisoned here for, what

is it, a month?' Ross asked.

'Three weeks,' said Fliss. 'Golly, I hope we all pass the examination.'

'If Maggie has anything to do with it, you will.' Ross eyed the menu board. 'She doesn't do failure. I'm for cottage pie today. I suppose you girls are on rabbit food?'

'I should be,' said Cora. 'Our landlady's a superb cook and insists we need to keep our strength up.'

'You'll be worked hard,' said Ross. 'Walking around with books balanced on your head and climbing out of aircraft windows. You'll have great fun. Apart from warning you not to eat doughnuts, has Maggie told you that doing the pilots' laundry is an important part of the course?'

'Don't believe a word he says,' another amused voice chipped in.

'Cullen, you old devil,' said Ross. 'I thought you were ferrying lobsters from Norway to Newcastle?'

'I have been. Trust you to find the prettiest two girls in the queue. The name's Tony, by the way.' He smiled at the girls.

'I'm keeping Fliss and Cora company while we wait for our chow,' said Ross. 'Maggie always puts her trainees on a lettuce-leaf diet. Lord knows why.'

'I saw your name down for the simulator,' said Tony. 'How did it go?'

The pilots' conversation became like ancient Greek to Cora. Fliss rolled her eyes at her and the queue inched forward. The girls accepted portions of cottage pie and vegetables. Tony Cullen, Cora noticed, opted for macaroni cheese with chips plus at least half a ton of peas and carrots.

'He's vegetarian,' said Ross, edging closer as they waited to pay.

She ignored the tingle running down her spine. Even with the savoury smell of minced beef in the air, she could detect the fresh, lemony scent of the first officer's aftershave.

'May we share your table?' he asked. 'We promise not to talk shop. Scout's honour!'

Cora bit her lip. 'I expect the other girls will wonder why we don't sit with them,' she said.

'You can't all fit on one table,' said Ross. 'Even with your sylphlike figures.'

Laughing, Cora turned her head to look up at him. His eyes met hers and she swallowed hard. Gripping her tray tightly, she prayed her bag wouldn't slip from her shoulder and create another major incident.

'So, you two, will you take pity on me and help keep this reprobate in order while we eat?' Tony beseeched Fliss and Cora.

'Why not?' Fliss stole a chip from his plate. 'Unless it's a frightful sin to fraternise with first officers on day one.'

* * *

'Determining etiquette is a necessary part of life and of your training,' said Maggie Martin after lunch. 'The captain and his first officer are very important but, given the passenger load, without a cabin attendant they aren't allowed to take off.' She nodded towards the girls who wouldn't be based full time at Gatwick. 'Some of you will operate solo because the DC3 aeroplane needs only one stewardess. But if you're crewed on the Elizabethan, you'll be the number two hostess and your number one will be in charge.'

Someone's hand shot up. 'Do we wait on the crew as well as the passengers?'

Miss Martin grinned. 'Believe me, you won't want pilots searching for snacks and untidying your galley.' Laughter rippled round the room. 'Always serve the flight deck crew first. They're your priority. You can read up on cabin service this evening, ready for a quiz tomorrow.' She glared at them. 'The reputation of the airline depends on you. If your cabin service is sloppy and your attitude's flippant, the passengers will feel dissatisfied, and rightly so. If a flight's delayed or there's turbulence, your calm presence will reassure them.' She noticed Fliss's hand waving.

'Do you have a question, Felicity?'

'Yes, please, Miss Martin. How much actual practice do we have?'

Maggie smiled. 'I can't let you loose on real passengers until you're checked out as competent. Tomorrow at ten o'clock we're off to do circuits and bumps, but we'll remain belted into our seats for the twenty minutes or so we're airborne. Don't worry. By the time I've finished with you, you'll all be capable of serving lunch to her majesty Queen Elizabeth herself.'

Cora could have sworn she detected a tiny wink in Fliss's direction. Despite the chief hostess's ice-cool demeanour, she possessed a sense of humour.

'Regarding the flight deck, who do you serve first?'

'The captain,' muttered most people.

'What if his first officer's a woman?'

The responses differed.

'The captain's always served first,' said Maggie. 'This airline has two female first officers, but no way do you treat them as anything other than aircrew.'

Cora shifted in her seat. With so much to learn, so much to remember, would she ever earn her golden wing? Were the others feeling as dejected?

'You're looking uneasy, Cora, and several others.' Maggie's gaze swept their faces. 'If ever you're on duty and feel everything's against you, take a deep breath and tell yourself you can get through whatever situation's worrying you. Your training's designed to help you do this and I wouldn't have selected any of you, had I not been certain I was picking the right girl for the job. All of you are entering a very different world from your usual one. You need to concentrate hard for these next weeks, and when we've reached the end and you've passed your exam, that's when the real challenge begins.' She fixed them with that glare which, Cora realised, indicated Maggie's bark was much worse than her bite.

★ ★ ★

'What exactly are circuits and bumps?'

'Taking off, landing again and doing the whole thing over and over,' said Cora, negotiating frosty pavements. 'I wish I hadn't forgotten to pack my furry boots. We could be in for some wintry weather.'

'I didn't pack boots, either. Just think, if we were like the Honourable Miss Fliss Fenton-Grey, we could ring our parents and ask them to send the chauffeur with whatever we needed. Don't you know?'

'You know, Wendy,' said Cora, grabbing a lamp-post, 'Fliss is all right. She can't help her posh background.'

'Whoops!' Wendy hung on to Cora's arm. 'I can't help thinking she's got her eye on a four-ringer for a husband. Those debby types must get bored to tears with the kind of young men they meet at dances and parties.'

'From the little I know about her, she's as determined as you and me to make a go of things. If all she's after is a husband, I imagine her father could find her a handsome young lieutenant.'

'While you were lunching yesterday,' said Wendy, 'she was definitely fluttering her eyelashes at First Officer Anderson.'

'Ross is engaged to be married,' said Cora a little too quickly.

'Really? To an air hostess?'

'No. He told us his fiancée is French and training to become a doctor. Her name's Nicole and she lives in Paris. Goodness, it's cold. Do you think we could fly to the Mediterranean for our circuits and bumps?'

Wendy narrowed her eyes. 'First Officer Anderson seems rather flirtatious for an engaged man, don't you think?'

'It's none of our business.'

'Yesterday I got the distinct impression he couldn't take his eyes off you.'

'What rubbish! Anyway, we're here to train as airhostesses. If a hostess gets married, once that ring's on her finger, she loses her job. Grounded. How silly would that be?'

'Point taken. We're nearly there. I've only flown once before, so I can't help feeling excited. How about you?'

'Same here,' said Cora. 'Do you think Maggie will serve us coffee during our flight?'

'Even she has to be strapped in. Maybe they're trying to scare us before they waste money on training someone who'll need smelling salts if turbulence strikes.'

* * *

'Remember, everyone,' said Maggie when everyone assembled in Room 12. 'You're in safe hands. The captain will carry out a routine check on one of the first officers and before we take off, I'll carry out the pre-flight passenger briefing. Please listen and react like perfect passengers should!' Her eyes twinkled. 'Anyone who pushes the hostess call button will be making morning coffees for the rest of the week. Now, follow me.'

Cora snuggled her chin inside her scarf as a wind straight from Siberia sliced across the tarmac. Maggie led them to the Elizabethan in its bright red and white Castle Airways livery and they kept in an orderly group, watching for hazards like forklift trucks and airport personnel pushing wheeled steps and baggage trolleys.

Every girl gazed up at the two pilots visible through the windscreen, each wearing headphones. The captain raised his hand to Maggie, displaying four shiny gold rings on his jacket sleeve, while the younger one talked to someone Cora presumed must be sitting in the control tower.

'That first officer looks about fourteen,' Wendy whispered.

Maggie climbed the steps and stood beside the doorway. As each girl boarded, she greeted her, instructing everyone to sit beside a window and strap herself in. Cora heard the engines roar into life and soon she felt the big bird ease forward while Maggie, hidden from sight in the galley, switched on the PA system.

'Good morning, ladies. Captain French and his crew welcome you aboard this Castle Airways check flight, during which a number of controlled circuits and landings will take place. I would remind you not to unfasten your seatbelts. Please take time to familiarise yourself with the location of the emergency exits . . . '

Cora noted the chief hostess's unhurried delivery and shivered with anticipation, imagining herself as the one speaking into a microphone. She realised why Maggie had instructed them all to sit alone. This was a time to absorb the cabin's atmosphere from a passenger's point of view. When the aircraft taxied to a halt, Cora received an impression of a giant bird tiptoeing at the runway's edge. Hearing the engines revving, she felt a rush of excitement and couldn't wait to be airborne.

She felt her body thrust against the

back of her seat as they raced down the runway. The aircraft lifted and Cora, nose practically pressed against the window, looked down upon miniature aeroplanes and toy town buildings shrinking further as the plane gained height.

Soon the aircraft banked and began its descent. Cora longed to be on the flight deck, listening to air traffic control. The floor seemed to rise and meet the soles of her shoes as they lost height. She watched those tiny houses and toy cars magnify until the aircraft skimmed hedges and fences and its tyres kissed the runway in a perfect landing.

The engines roared and they were up and away again. Cora gasped, again experiencing the full-throttle thrust. She looked around guiltily in case anyone was laughing at her but couldn't help feeling like a joyful child in a swing boat.

When they landed for the final time, she wondered how many marks out of ten the young pilot had scored. His face had looked the colour of putty when she gazed up at him from the tarmac. But that was hardly surprising, considering the huge metal beast he was about to coax off the ground.

★ ★ ★

'That silvery-blue eye shadow looks good on you, Cora.'

Cora blinked at her reflection. 'Really?'

'It's vivid but not garish,' said Fliss.

'Sitting here surrounded by lipsticks and lotions is much more fun than sliding down a chute on a freezing cold day.'

'Where's your sense of adventure?' Fliss chuckled. 'One or two of the others looked a bit worried, don't you think?'

'I overheard one say she'd applied to be an air hostess, not a flipping commando!'

'She obviously didn't take notice of

what Miss Martin said about our true purpose,' said Fliss. 'I'm loving this, you know, Cora. Enjoying every fantastic, frightening moment of it. How about you?'

'Ditto,' said Cora. 'When I had to explain how to fasten a seatbelt, it seemed such an obvious thing. But as I completed each little action, I realised how vital attention to detail is. We need to react by instinct.'

'You're a model trainee, darling. You have a divine speaking voice and you're the perfect shape for a stewardess. Passengers will adore you.'

'It's nice of you to say so, Fliss, but I don't think I'm any different from anyone else. Probably a bit clumsier if truth were known.'

'Why do you say that? This morning, when Miss Martin lifted her arm just as you walked past with those empty trays, you dodged her very skilfully.'

'I expected her to play a trick on me,' said Cora. 'It was self-preservation.'

'It's something to be wary of, isn't it?

Like passengers' feet and elbows turning the gangway into an obstacle course.'

'That's where I'll need to watch out,' said Cora. 'My mother used to say I was the type of child to trip over a matchstick.'

'But look where you are now. Halfway through training to become an air stewardess . . . Hey, I'd better go. I'm next in line for eyebrow plucking.' Fliss glided away, leaving a trail of Chanel Number 5.

Cora doubted the beautician would find even one stray hair. Fliss was the kind of young woman who'd look as spick and span handing out boiled sweets as she would gracing the enclosure at Ascot or taking tea at a smart London hotel.

5

A few days later the trainees visited the catering premises, only to be taken aback by the sight of so many meals being prepared, even though the package holiday season wasn't yet in full swing. Each girl tried putting together a cold roast meat and salad portion.

'Ladies, I applaud your ingenuity,' said their guide. 'But think what might happen when trays are loaded into containers. Pretty piles of carrot sticks will collapse. Neat rolls of ham will unroll. We must think realistic, not artistic. Turbulence is your worst enemy — so no placing the Danish pastry near the beetroot salad.'

As everyone headed back to the Beehive, Cora noticed two Castle hostesses walking towards their waiting aircraft. They'd tied silky white head-scarves over their forage caps to avoid the wind whipping their hats away, and both waved cheerfully to the chief hostess and her chicks.

'They're working a Gatwick to Cannes service,' said Maggie, opening the door. 'The number one, Jeanne Whitfield, is a check hostess, so you'll come across her sooner or later. And don't look so crestfallen,' she added once they were inside Room 12. 'Some of you'll soon be off to Mediterranean resorts. Now go and have lunch, but be back at two o'clock so you can show the instructor how skilled you are at applying a triangular bandage.'

Cora and Wendy entered the cafeteria together. Wendy pointed to a big table. 'I'll keep that for us if you get me something to eat.'

When Cora returned with their food, Wendy drew her attention to the end of the queue. 'I spy your friendly first officer. He whom you ambushed in the corridor our first day?'

'Yes, I do remember, thanks very much.' Cora toyed with her chicken salad as a few more from their group pulled out chairs.

'Give him a wave, then. He's looking our way.'

'I'll do no such thing. He'll think I want him to sit with us.'

'Too late. I'm waving instead. Otherwise he'll tell all the other pilots the Bristol girls are stuck up. Besides, he has the looks of Robert Redford. What more could a girl ask?'

'You really are hopeless,' said Cora, sneaking a glance at the food counter where Ross Anderson loaded his tray. She willed herself not to blush when he approached.

'May I join you?' He smiled around at everyone.

'Pull out a chair,' said Wendy.

Ross put down his tray beside her. 'Phew. I'd rather fly four tons of metal around than carry one of these, any day.'

Cora noted his plate of steak and kidney pie with chips and peas, plus a portion of jam roly-poly and custard.

'Are you stoking up ready to fly, or have you just landed?'

'I'm on a positioning flight at three,' he said, tucking his serviette in his collar. 'We're taking an empty Dakota to Liverpool, night-stopping then flying a load of football supporters to Hamburg first thing tomorrow.'

'Will you be able to watch the game? Wendy asked. 'My dad used to take me to matches when I was little and I still go with him sometimes.'

'Sounds like you don't have a brother.'

'Correct,' said Wendy. 'I'm a one-off.'

'Me too,' said Cora.

'That makes three of us then. Probably all spoilt rotten,' said Ross cheerfully.

'That's a cliché,' said Wendy. 'But I asked you a question.'

'I'll be spending any free time with the crew,' said Ross. 'I'm not a great football fan. Prefer rugby.'

'We went on board a Dakota yesterday. Familiarisation,' said Cora.

'No circuits and bumps?' He smiled at her.

Why did her tummy perform back-flips when he looked at her with those blue, blue eyes? 'None since our trip in the Elizabethan.'

'Ah, the Lizzie's great but the old Dakota's my favourite.'

'So you fly both?'

'Yep.' Ross took a gulp of water. 'I'm filling in here and there these days, but I'll know soon where I'm to be based.'

'Maybe you'll come to Bristol!' Wendy twirled a copper ringlet around her index finger. Cora kept her eyes fixed on her food.

'The crews based at the smaller airports are like families,' said Ross. 'That's one of the good things.'

'And the bad things?'

He looked at Cora, as if weighing up his answer. 'It's not a bad thing, of course, but some pilots prefer more variety. Unless there's a charter flight, you two will mostly shuttle up and down country on the domestic routes.'

'I don't care,' said Cora. 'Miss Martin says some passengers fly so regularly, we'll end up being shown snaps of their children.'

'It'll seem weird though,' said Wendy. 'Hardly ever seeing each other after spending several weeks together on the course.'

'Yes, you'll each take turns being queen bee of the DC3,' said Ross.

'Taking turns to get up at the crack of dawn on a Monday while the other one works a Tuesday,' said Wendy.

'Long day on, short day off as we catch up with our sleep,' said Cora.

'And soon it'll be the holiday season. Oh dear, I hope I don't get muddled and turn up on the wrong morning,' said Wendy.

'Doubtful.' Ross ploughed his fork into succulent pastry crust. 'You'll soon adjust. It's a strange life, in a way. In another, it's a rewarding one.'

'Did you always want to become a pilot?' Cora asked.

He chewed thoughtfully. 'When I was

five, I wanted to be a pirate.' He ducked as Wendy mock-punched him. 'OK. I honestly can't remember when I didn't want to fly aeroplanes.'

'What did your parents think about that?'

A shadow crossed his face. 'My father lost his life in the war. I was born in 1940 and I was just three years old when his plane was shot down.'

'I'm so sorry.' Wendy bit her lip. 'I didn't mean to pry.'

'It's fine. Sadly, I have very little recall of him, but my mother kept lots of photographs. She remarried when I was eleven and luckily I've always got on well with my stepfather.'

'My dad was in the RAF during the war and afterwards,' said Cora. 'He was one of the lucky ones.'

'Life's a lottery.' Ross kept his eyes on his plate.

Cora glanced at the clock above the counter. 'We must go, Wendy.' She scrabbled under the table for her handbag just as the first officer stretched out one long leg. Her fingers brushed his ankle and she drew back as if she'd been stung. 'I'm so sorry,' she said.

'My fault for taking up too much space. See you down the route, girls. Good luck with your exam, though I'm sure you'll pass with flying colours.'

Cora and Wendy hurried along the corridors towards Room 12.

'You two seem to make a habit of apologising to one another,' said Wendy.

'It's me and handbags,' said Cora. 'Thank goodness I shan't need to carry one during cabin service.'

'Don't change the subject. Didn't you notice something odd about that conversation?'

'The fact that we're all only children? Doesn't that make us independent types — the sort who'd want to work in aviation?'

'I didn't mean that. I'm wondering why Ross didn't mention his fiancée even though he talked about his late father and his mother.'

'We were on a short meal break, making conversation without getting indigestion.'

'Hmm,' said Wendy. 'If you say so.'

'Did you notice they had treacle sponge on the menu? If we'd had more time, I doubt I could've resisted that.'

'At this moment, First Officer Robert Redford's probably scoffing his jam roly-poly and looking forward to a slice of treacle sponge for afters.'

★ ★ ★

Ross Anderson pushed aside his left-over portion of pudding. He must be slipping. Normally he cast a casual eye over any new hostess intake and watched his peers develop yearnings, crushes and occasionally meaningful relationships. A spot of flirtation, a bit of banter with a jolly girl like Wendy Baker — who'd make a terrific younger sister — was as far as he was ever prepared to let himself go. Shielded by

Nicole, his Parisian fiancée, Ross remained focused on his main objective: enhanced skills and experience. More air miles in his logbook.

His far-off fiancée helped enormously. Nicole rescued him from invitations to make up foursomes, and one mention of her deflected any come-hither looks received not only from stewardesses but also from passengers. His mother had told him he looked good in uniform, like his father had done, she'd added with a wistful smile. Ross remained unaware how attractive he was to women, but feared someone with her eye on the main chance making a play for him simply because he was a pilot. If he slipped Nicole's name into the conversation, nobody questioned her existence. Why should they?

But Cora Murray had slipped beneath his radar. Or rather, she'd knocked him off course, and the way he felt didn't fit his plans for the future. How stupid was that? That time he'd shared a table with

Cora and Fliss, he blurted out something about his last visit to Paris to see his fiancée. They probably thought he considered himself a prize catch if he felt the need to declare himself unavailable to potential husband-hunters. Cora's subsequent coolness towards him was painfully evident. If ever they ended up crewed together, would the sparks fly?

'Penny for 'em!'

Ross looked up guiltily, as if his thoughts filled a cartoon speech bubble above his head. 'Tony,' he said. 'Macaroni man himself! Pull up a chair. I've got half an hour before I have to file my flight plan.'

* * *

The written exam was the trainees' final hurdle. Each had passed the first-aid course and could fasten a seat belt with her eyes shut. Jeanne Whitfield, the blonde check hostess newly appointed as Maggie Martin's deputy, oversaw them.

Jeanne looked around at them all. 'Don't be nervous. We want you to succeed and you'll find nothing you haven't already learnt, so don't worry. Please turn over your papers now.'

Cora scanned the questions. She could do this. She really could. She must! She wrote her name on her paper and in her mind's eye, walked herself down the Dakota's aisle. At the five-minute warning, she'd just stopped writing.

Afterwards, she headed straight for Wendy's table. 'What did you think of it?'

'Not as bad as I'd anticipated,' said the redhead. 'I've probably done OK but I'm not counting my chickens.'

Suddenly Cora felt an inexplicable surge of longing to see Ross. Wendy brimmed with suggestions as to what they might do with the rest of the day, as they weren't taking the Bristol train until next morning. But all Cora could think about was the golden-haired first officer and how much he'd impressed her with his attitude to his career. Of course, there couldn't be any other reason to wish for his company. Could there?

'So, do you fancy trying for tickets to see *Oliver*?'

Cora realised Wendy's chatter had progressed to the point where she expected a decision. 'Um, tonight you mean?'

'Yes, of course. We can ring our landlady and tell her we'll be really late back. Who knows when we'll be so close to London again?'

'All right. But only if we're both checked out and deserve a celebration.'

'We'll find out soon. Let's hope we can celebrate with a nice tea somewhere. I fancy iced buns.'

'I daren't,' said Cora. 'How dreadful if we passed the exam but couldn't fit into our uniforms?'

★   ★   ★

Cora moved into her new abode on the Sunday. Her father drove her together with a hotchpotch of possessions. She gathered up bags of groceries while her dad hauled her luggage from the boot.

'Your mum's making sure you don't starve, that's for sure. Serves you right for not staying for Sunday dinner.'

'I keep telling her I need to watch what I eat. Our landlady was just as bad.'

'You'll soon work it off,' said Roy Murray. 'You're going to do a good job, lass.'

Cora caught her breath. Her father hardly ever used that term of affection.

'You remembered to check out the bus timetable for the morning?'

'I did, thanks, Dad. You never know, in the evening I might get a lift back with one of the crew.' A thrill of pride rippled through her.

When they reached her first-floor room, Cora unlocked the door and stepped inside, holding her breath. 'This primrose paint is lovely,' she said.

Roy cleared his throat.

'Sorry, Dad. Put the cases down and

85

we'll have a look around.'

'We won't need a tour guide, that's for sure.'

'It's just the right size for me.'

'You'll be snug as a bug in a rug.' He cast an eye around and nodded. 'Do you know what? I think I'll leave you to get sorted. You don't need me under your feet.'

'Thanks for everything, Dad. You know the number of the hall phone?'

He patted his top pocket. 'Sure you're all right for cash?'

'Positive. I'll walk down with you.'

After she climbed back up to her bedsit, the smell of fresh paint still lingering, Cora hugged herself with glee. It was great to have her parents close and handy, but this big step excited her. She'd enjoyed the training course and Wendy's company, but she was ready for her taste of independence.

Cora arranged food in the small fridge and cupboards. She unpacked her cases, positioned plump patchwork cushions around, and wished she'd got her dad to hang her white paper lantern shade. At dusk she drew the curtains, turned on the light and switched on her new radio, knowing her parents would be listening to *Sing Something Simple*. Her mum had sent a home-cooked dinner on an enamel plate, ready to warm in her Baby Belling. Her tummy rumbled at the thought of chicken with sausage meat and fresh parsley stuffing.

'Here's to my new life!' She raised a glass of lemonade to herself.

6

The alarm jangled. Cora's hand shot out to silence the shrillness. Where was she? For a moment, she expected to see Wendy's copper curls on the snowy pillow in the other twin bed.

'Oh, my goodness.' The big day had arrived. She switched on the bedside lamp and swung her legs from under the covers, ignoring the morning chill.

When she let herself out of the front door, she hardly noticed the wintry gloom. Soon she sat on the bus, listening to the cheerful chatter of cleaning ladies and shift workers already on board. Five minutes before her check-in time, she stood in front of the brightly lit Castle Airways desk.

'May I help you?' A uniformed receptionist looked up with the perfect proportion of cheerfulness for early morning. 'Hello! I saw your name and

Wendy's on the roster. Congrats on getting the job.'

'Thanks, Linda. I'm still feeling stunned. But what's this? Castle Airways recruited you too?'

'I fancied a change so I applied for a ground job. Now, come on through and meet the station manager. It's just him and me on duty. Your number one's already here. This is Helen's last week flying out of Bristol because she's based at Gatwick from now on.'

Cora followed the ground hostess into the big office filled with filing cabinets, desks, telephones and a strange machine rattling typescript on to a fat roll of paper. A uniformed man, phone glued to his ear, gave her a friendly wave.

'Hello, Cora.' Helen held out her hand and Cora grabbed it as if clutching a life belt. 'I'm afraid your uniform hasn't arrived yet but I gather it's being put on the next available aircraft.'

'I thought I'd better wear a suit. This

is the plainest I have.'

'That navy blue is perfect.'

Cora wished the butterflies in her tummy would shuck off their hobnailed boots.

'I picked up your roster.' Helen held out a brown envelope. 'You'll need to collect it from your pigeonhole mid-week ready for the following week. You're working with me again on Thursday. It's the Rotterdam service so I can make sure you're OK with duty-free restrictions and such.'

'Thank you,' said Cora, trying to look confident.

'Believe me, if you've passed muster in Maggie's eyes, you'll be fine. Now, let's check our supplies. We have 20 passengers joining here and we pick up again at Cardiff.'

When it was time to board, they hurried across to the Dakota standing, steps in place and door open.

'Brrrr! I shall miss this aircraft but I can't say dear old Pappa's the warmest of beasties,' said Helen. 'Why don't you check the seatbelts are tidy? I'll check we've got everything.'

Cora set off up the sloping cabin and began checking from the front, moving back towards the tiny galley.

'Good,' said Helen. 'By the time we leave Cardiff there'll be plenty of hot water. Captain Crosby's here so his first officer must be around somewhere. I'm not sure who it is because of this spring change-around.'

So her first flight was to be captained by the famous Bing. A tall figure hurried up the steps, broad shoulders blocking out most of the light as he stood in the doorway. Cora's first impression of Bing was of a man with kind eyes, grizzled hair and a ginger moustache.

'Good morning, Helen,' he said. 'And you, young lady, must be Cora?'

She held out her hand. 'That's right, Captain Crosby. I apologise for not being in uniform. Helen says it's arriving soon.'

'As I hope my first officer will be.'

Bing set off towards the cockpit, calling over one shoulder, 'Have you seen young Cullen this morning, Helen?'

'T . . . Tony? Not yet, Captain Crosby.'

'There's someone coming now,' said Cora, peering through the open door. 'It looks like First Officer Cullen.'

Helen smoothed down her hair, reached inside her handbag and pulled out a scent bottle. She dabbed some behind her ears. 'I thought it was unlike Tony to be late.'

Cora caught a whiff of Hartnell's 'In Love' and wondered if it was for the benefit of the passengers or the first officer. Helen's cheeks were far rosier than they had been.

'So you've already met Tony?' Helen reached for a bag of boiled sweets and tipped a pile onto a tiffin tray.

'Wendy Baker and I shared a table with him and his friend, Ross, in the cafeteria on our first day.'

'Our paths hardly ever cross nowadays,' said Helen.

Tony bounded up the steps. 'Two

hostesses on a DC3 — oh my goodness, how can that be?'

'Hello, Tony. Cora's doing her first flight with me today but don't expect two lots of refreshments.'

Tony smiled down at her. 'You know very well first officers have hollow legs.' He turned to Cora. 'So you made it? Congratulations. Though it'll be a cold day in hell when Maggie Martin picks a wrong un.'

Cora jumped as an impatient buzz resounded through the cabin.

'Probably Bing chasing you?' Helen raised her eyebrows.

Tony set off, hoisting his briefcase on one shoulder. Halfway along, he turned around. 'Most importantly, the captain and I are custard cream fans.'

'We'll bear that in mind,' said Helen.

Everything seemed to kaleidoscope for Cora. A few minutes later the passengers were heading their way, Linda leading them across the tarmac. Helen greeted them with a cheerful 'Good morning', sometimes addressing a passenger by name. Cora waited at the rear. When everyone was seated, she set off up the cabin, offering sweets and checking seatbelts were secured. She didn't even notice the aircraft begin taxiing, so intent was she on her duties.

'I've done a head check,' said Helen. 'I'll do the pre-flight announcement while you go back and strap yourself in. We'll swap over for the Cardiff departure.'

With no public address system on this aircraft, Helen was obliged to compete with the formidable rumble of the engines. She disappeared through the cockpit door to give the thumbs-up that the cabin was secured, and soon they were airborne and off went the seatbelt sign.

They left Cardiff, Cora having completed her first on-board flight announcement without fluffing her lines. Helen gave her a few tips but Cora found her duties hectic enough with someone else helping her. How on earth would she cope alone with a full load?

'You're probably wondering how you'll manage on your own,' said her mentor, reading Cora's mind. 'You'll get faster with practice.'

'I hope so,' said Cora, ready to set off down the cabin again. Smiling came easily. Wasn't she at last performing the job she'd dreamed of?

★   ★   ★

At Newcastle there were more new faces and more familiar uniforms. The skipper and his crew caught a bus into Newcastle, Captain Crosby greeting the conductor like an old friend.

'The bus crews are used to us turning up,' said Helen as they trundled through the countryside. 'I want to pop into the Fenwicks store. Keep me company if you like. I expect the crew will go to a news cinema after lunch. You'll find pilots have a massive capacity for cartoon shows as well as food.'

Cora peppered Helen with questions. She'd jumped all the hoops towards earning her single wing, but knowing all the whys and wherefores of the role was another matter.

At the restaurant, Captain Crosby asked questions about Bristol. He'd requested the posting because his wife wanted to move closer to her parents' home. 'I'm going to become a west-country boy,' he said, putting on an atrocious accent. 'We've taken a flat while we house hunt.' He frowned. 'For the life of me I can't remember the name of the road, though I know how to drive there.'

Everyone laughed.

'I've found a flat share,' said Tony. 'Someone who operates an air taxi firm put the word round he had a room going.'

'How about you, Cora? Local girl I imagine?'

'Not local enough to live at home, Captain Crosby,' she said. 'I'm renting a bedsit in Clifton. It's newly renovated.'

'We'll be near neighbours,' said Tony.

'I'm living just off Whiteladies Road.'

Before Cora could respond, Captain Crosby butted in. 'You can call me James, Cora. But most people call me Bing. Now, whatever you do, don't divulge your address to First Officer Cullen. Before you know it, he'll be bringing round his shirts for you to iron.'

Again everyone laughed, though Cora sensed Helen's chuckle was a tad strained. Without a doubt, the senior hostess had feelings for curly-haired Tony Cullen, and in his company found it difficult to keep her eyes off him. How ironic it must be, knowing she'd got the posting she'd longed for, with the prospect of more trips to the continent, only to find the object of her attentions was now based at the airport she was about to quit.

Helen brought up the subject of the new postings. 'So who's the other half of the Bristol crew?'

'Ah, my opposite number's Captain Tracey, arguably the best pilot we have, though please don't quote me on that. George flew in the war and the DC3's his second home, so he's delighted with this posting. But his wife doesn't want to leave their abode — not surprising, as they have a beautiful Regency house near Brighton. George will probably find a modest hotel and do some commuting if I know him.'

'I haven't heard a thing on the grapevine about his first officer,' said Tony. He turned to Cora. 'In case you don't know, you could be stuck with Bing and me for the foreseeable future.'

Captain Crosby shrugged. 'They might slot chaps in temporarily with George for now. He might even get a woman.'

Cora's lips twitched and she hurriedly pressed her serviette to her mouth. Captain Crosby struck her as a kindly, gentlemanly person, but he'd sounded a little bit disapproving.

'Hopefully she'll keep you all in order, whoever she is,' said Helen.

'Just because you're going where the

glamour is, it's no excuse for being cheeky.' Tony wagged his finger at her.

'We've plenty of glamour of our own at Bristol,' said Bing.

'Yes, the Dakota has to be the Lauren Bacall of the airways,' said Cora. 'No one could say she's not glamorous.'

'Touché,' said Bing.

'Did you know Miss Bacall was born Betty Joan Perske? Tony chimed in. 'The question is, would she have been as successful, had she stuck to her own name?'

'I don't believe this,' said Bing. 'Is my first officer aiming to be Brain of Britain?'

⋆　⋆　⋆

Back at base, after two busy sectors, Tony Cullen offered a lift to both hostesses.

'Bing wants an early night,' he said. 'I'm happy to drive you back, but how about a quick drink first?'

Cora didn't like to confess how

drained she felt. She seemed to have been on her feet forever, despite hours of practice while working at Gigi's. They chatted with the steward in the quiet bar until Tony suggested the girls wait in the terminal building while he brought round his car. When they saw his headlights, the hostesses hurried outside and Cora chuckled to see the lanky first officer clambering out of a mini. She volunteered to sit in the back.

'OK then, Cora?' He pulled back the seat for her. 'Bet you wish you were flying to the sunshine instead of around the chilly UK?'

'Not at all. Everyone's been so friendly today. I'll enjoy seeing familiar faces once I get a few more trips under my belt.'

'I've enjoyed living in Bristol,' said Helen, settling beside Tony. 'But I'm looking forward to seeing different places.'

Cora sat quietly, listening to the other two chat. She noticed Helen shift gradually closer to Tony, until their shoulders were a heartbeat away from each other. Slowly he became less talkative until, on the edge of the city, he spoke.

'I think I'll drop you first, Helen. Then Cora can help navigate if I get lost finding my way back.'

'Whatever you think best.'

An understandable decision, thought Cora. But Helen's bleak tone spoke volumes.

★ ★ ★

Next day Cora received a phone call. Her landlord, who occupied the basement flat, caught her on the verge of going out.

'It's the airport for you, Miss Murray,' he said when she opened her door.

'Thank you, Mr Jelly.'

She dashed downstairs to pick up the phone. 'Cora speaking.'

'It's Linda. I thought you'd like to

know your uniform just flew in on a freighter. When are you on duty again?'

'Not till Thursday, but I'll come and collect it.'

'On your day off?'

Cora smiled down the phone. 'I can't wait to try it on.'

'If you can be here by one, we could have lunch together.'

'I'd like that,' said Cora. 'See you later.'

She hurried back upstairs, put on her camel coat and picked up a brown suede handbag. As she walked to the bus stop, a newsagent's placard caught her eye. Two of Britain's favourite actors, Roger Moore and Patrick McGoohan, were reported each to be earning £2000 per week. Cora made a face. Goodness, it made her £13 weekly wage look undernourished!

* * *

'I wouldn't swap though, would you? I love this job.' Linda bit into her egg sandwich after Cora reported the stars' earnings.

'It's taken me months to get this far, so I wouldn't give up now, that's for sure. As if I could ever act.'

'Don't you think we're on show when we're in uniform?'

'I'll tell you once I start wearing mine!'

'People on the bus often assume I'm an air hostess,' said Linda. 'Even though I don't have a gold wing on my lapel.'

'On Thursday I'll be able to compare notes.'

Linda's seat faced the entrance. 'You'll never guess who's just walked in.'

'Probably not, given I only know about two people at this airport,' said Cora.

'Tony Cullen's here. I wonder what he's up to on his day off.'

'Well he already has a uniform, so I've no idea.' Cora kept her head down. Whatever Tony was doing, she hated the thought of him sitting with her simply because they were crewed together. But, just as she'd taken a mouthful of cheese and chutney, the first officer appeared at her shoulder.

'Another one who can't keep away,' he teased. 'Hello, you two. Mind if I join you?'

Cora, catapulted back to the cafeteria that first day of her training course when Ross Anderson had accompanied Tony, nodded, her mouth still full.

'I've ordered plaice and chips.' Tony sat down. 'Speedily heading towards pilot's paunch unless I mend my wicked ways.'

'It's a bit of a drive just for fish and chips,' Cora couldn't resist teasing.

'I've been looking around my flat-mate's air taxi firm,' said Tony. 'Bill has two aircraft but needs another pilot to help out.'

'Don't you have enough flying to do already?' Linda asked.

'Yep. I just like looking at anything that flies.'

Linda laughed. 'I must go. There's a pile of tickets to be written out.'

Tony jumped to his feet.

'Enjoy your fish and chips,' said Linda. 'Don't let Cora leave without her cardboard box.'

'She's a nice girl,' said Tony, sitting back down as Linda hurried away.

'She was very kind when I arrived for my interview, quaking with fear.'

'How I hate interviews,' said Tony, shaking the ketchup bottle as his meal arrived. 'Hey, how about another coffee?'

'I haven't checked on bus times yet. I wasn't expecting to come here today but Linda rang about my uniform.'

'If you don't mind waiting for me to finish, you can ride back with me.'

She hesitated. 'OK. But let me get the coffees.'

'Busman's holiday?' Tony teased. 'I can't let you wait on me.' Ignoring her protests, he set off for the counter.

'I'd appreciate a word with you, Cora,' he said when he got back. 'It's personal.'

'Is this to do with yesterday? Did I do something awful on the flight?'

'Crikey, no. The absolute opposite, in fact. Bing said that for someone wet behind the ears, you seemed exceptionally calm and competent.'

'I was petrified! But I learnt a lot from Helen.'

He speared chips with his fork. 'I'll explain later.'

7

'Do you think you'll get on well with Bill as a flatmate?' Cora asked Tony as he drove.

'I expect so,' he said. 'We probably won't see much of each other.'

'That'd help,' said Cora. 'So, what did you want to say?'

He sighed. 'I'm hopeless at this kind of thing. I mustn't take up too much of your time but do you fancy a bit of a walk, maybe on the downs? I'll drop you off afterwards.'

Cora considered. Why not? Something bothered him and she was well aware aircrew found it difficult to have a social life. Her best friend from schooldays had married and moved to Cornwall and apart from Em, she'd formed no real friendships at Gigi's. The salesgirls probably never gave her a thought these days.

Tony glanced across at her.

'OK, then. Let's get some fresh air.'

Tony smacked his forehead. 'You've just begun a job where you'll be walking miles while we chaps sit on our behinds in the cockpit. Are you sure about walking?'

'I might just manage to totter a few yards.'

He shot her a wicked grin and drove on in friendly silence. Approaching the city, Cora pointed out a few landmarks and Tony, heading in the direction of Bristol Zoo, found a side road to park upon.

'Don't forget to lock up,' said Cora as they got out. 'Imagine if someone stole my new uniform.'

'Heaven forbid they should steal my precious mini.'

'Come on, let's head over there — towards the Cabot Tower.'

They fell into step, Tony with hands dug in the pockets of his duffel coat and Cora striding beside him, her hands in brown wool mittens. She wondered how much longer he'd wait before confiding his thoughts, though she'd a fair idea what this was about. She hadn't anticipated acting as an agony aunt along with all her other new duties.

'It's about Helen,' he said at last.

'Right.'

'I'm not sure how much you picked up yesterday but — oh crikey, this is so embarrassing!'

'Tony, just tell me what the problem is. I shan't judge you. It's not my business to do so.'

'OK. She and I were crewed together several times while we were both based at Manchester, so we ended up going to the same parties and so on. Nothing heavy. But at the farewell do we had after she got her Bristol posting, we both had a drink or two and, well, after a couple of smoochy dances, I found myself kissing her goodnight.'

'Oh dear. You were wearing your beer goggles — not that Helen's unattractive, of course,' said Cora.

'She's very attractive but she's not . . . I don't . . . '

'It's OK, you needn't spell it out,' said Cora gently. 'She'd like things to work out for the two of you but you don't feel the same.'

'Exactly. I found yesterday extremely awkward. Do you think I should buy her chocolates or whatever? To wish her well at Gatwick and all that.' He ran a hand through his curly brown hair.

Cora considered. 'Helen seemed taken aback you'd been posted here just as she was leaving, but she must realise you've had plenty of time to think. You didn't try to get in touch after she left Manchester, I take it?'

He shook his head. 'Nope. I knew our paths would cross some time, but I hate to think of her being miserable, carrying a torch for someone who doesn't feel the same way.'

'It's not your fault, Tony. But perhaps you could write her a letter or take her out for tea and tell her you're sorry if you gave her the wrong impression. Are you crewed together tomorrow?'

'Yes, and the day after on the Rotterdam service.'

'I'm doing that one too. My last before they let me loose on my own.'

Tony hesitated. 'I wonder if I should wait until then. What if I say something tomorrow and it upsets her? It'd be better if you were around, just in case.'

'That's up to you,' said Cora. 'My guess is, deep down she knows you're not interested, but when you come into her orbit you light a little flame inside her.'

'Cripes,' said Tony. 'I'm glad we're having this conversation. I feel braver now.'

Cora laughed. 'It sounds strange to hear that from a man who flies all over the place with countless people trusting him to get them to and fro safely.'

'Believe me, Miss Murray, I'm much better handling several tons of metal than I am handling eight or nine stones of femininity.'

'It's a good job I don't have a crush

on you then, isn't it?'

'My loss,' he said.

She knew he was joking.

'Come on,' he said. 'Let me take you to the zoo. We've got time for a look round, if we hurry.'

'Why the zoo?'

'Because I haven't visited a zoo since I was eleven. How about you?'

'Probably nine in my case.'

'OK. Let's go and see if we can spot any of the pilots among the gorillas.'

Cora chuckled. She was enjoying the fresh air and the banter. Being with Tony felt like being with the older brother she'd always wished she had.

*　*　*

Taking advantage of her non-hectic first week, Cora headed for the shops next day. She hadn't been able to resist trying on her new uniform after Tony dropped her off around eight p.m. the previous evening. He'd taken her out for a meal, having insisted, saying it was a good opportunity, neither being in uniform and so able to enjoy a glass of wine. He was good company and they shared the same taste in films, especially James Bond. Tony even offered to collect her next time she was on duty, so she needn't take the bus.

'You're very kind but I think it best if I say no.'

His cheeks had reddened. 'Is this because you're worried Helen might see us walk in together?'

'It's not that. Truly, I'm happy using the bus.'

'At least write down our flat's phone number,' he'd said. 'Just in case you ever need a lift.'

Now she stood at the cosmetics counter, telling the beautician about the demonstration she'd attended. The saleswoman found the items required and included more free samples.

Cora, wafting gardenia and freesia, purchased plain white gloves and spare pairs of stockings. Helen had warned of the hazards of seat belt straps dangling over arm rests, their buckles snagging fine nylons as the unsuspecting hostess passed by. She also booked a hairdresser's appointment for Friday. Her new Cilla Black style needed trimming, or else her dark locks wouldn't clear her collar, and she didn't want to incur Jeanne Whitfield's displeasure should the check hostess turn up on one of Cora's flights.

Like a genie popping from a lamp, Ross Anderson catapulted into her mind, though the attraction she felt still concerned her. The first officer had a fiancée. Even if he hadn't, the last thing Cora needed was a new relationship. How many other girls had she outshone on her way to seizing this chance? She couldn't be so stupid as to throw it all away because of a sudden crush on a blue-eyed, golden-haired, gorgeous young pilot.

That glow when Ross moved closer to her in the lunch queue and she was hit by the tang of lemon aftershave still lodged in her consciousness, though she doubted the first officer gave her a thought once out of her orbit. How lucky was she, being crewed with two kind, sensible men like Bing and Tony? What more could a girl ask?

★ ★ ★

Next morning, Cora turned a few heads on the bus journey to the airport, where she headed for the ladies' room to check her appearance in the full-length mirror. A stranger stared back. Her cap perched firmly on her head thanks to a discreet hairgrip. The Peter Pan collar of her powder-blue blouse peeped from beneath her slate-blue fitted jacket and pencil skirt. She'd managed not to ladder her nylons on the way and her navy blue court shoes gleamed.

Back in the office, Ted, the station manager, put down the phone and greeted her as if he'd never seen her wearing anything else but uniform.

''Morning, Cora. I'm afraid Helen's

called in sick, so you're on your own today.'

Cora stared back at him, her stomach looping the loop to end all loops. 'That's terrible. I mean, I'm so sorry Helen's poorly.'

'She said to tell you she has a migraine and daren't risk flying. She also told me she'd every confidence in you. Thought you did a good job on your first trip.' Ted bent over his paperwork.

Cora's heartbeat was taking lessons from her stomach. What if this had something to do with Helen's feelings for Tony? What an awful shame for her. But selfishly, Cora worried about herself. Would she remember everything? What if she got lost at Rotterdam Airport, an unfamiliar place with planes from many countries flying in and out?

'What's up?' Tony dumped his bags on the nearby table.

'Helen's not fit to fly today.'

'Oh, lordy, I hope this isn't my fault.'

'She has a migraine. I'd better hop to

it as I'm solo hostess.'

'Piece of cake. See you on board.' He picked up his bags, called a cheery good morning to the ground staff and headed off, mind obviously focused on his job. Cora reminded herself she should do the same.

Aboard the aircraft, she looked around the cabin. Suddenly she knew she was ready for this. Maybe it was all about wearing a uniform, but she felt she'd put on a different face today. And it felt good.

'Well, you're a sight for sore eyes.' The captain appeared in the doorway. 'Got your uniform, I see.'

'Thank goodness. With no Helen, the passengers might've thought I was any old person turning up to serve them.'

'Hmm. Sorry about Helen, but you'll just get on with the job, won't you?' Bing started up the aisle, then stopped and called, 'Remind me to buy Dutch waffles today, Cora. My wife has a sweet tooth.'

'Me too! So I shan't forget.'

Through the windows Cora saw ground crew moving about. The aircraft was connected to a generator and its tyres were wedged securely. Soon the luggage would be loaded. Every flight was the result of numerous procedures, small or large, but all vital. She watched Tony circling the DC3, carrying out his checks too.

Most of Cora's passengers were businessmen, but there was a mother travelling with her baby daughter so Cora suggested the woman sit in a rear seat. She reached overhead for a soft blue blanket, which the woman accepted gratefully, wrapping herself and her baby inside a warm cocoon. The baby cried on take-off, but Cora reassured the mother this would help prevent discomfort to the little one's ears. 'She's far too young to suck a fruit drop,' she said. 'Best let her cry.'

A flight engineer joined the crew at Liverpool and after landing at Rotter-dam, he escorted Cora to the catering section and bonded store. Part of her role was to check the duty-free goods the aircraft carried for sale. She enjoyed coffee in the airport as the four of them found a table next to an Aer Lingus crew. While the men talked about boring things, Cora and the two Irish hostesses compared notes about uniform, expenses and many topics she hadn't known anything about until joining Castle. She didn't reveal this was her first solo flight and hoped she hadn't tried to appear more sophisticated than she was.

The Irish crew were heading back to Dublin. 'See you down the route,' called their captain in his gorgeous brogue as they left.

Bing suggested lunch in the flying club. 'You'll know how to get there if you're ever left on your own,' he told Cora. 'Usually we look out for one another. Or, like today, you may find other airline crews to chat to.'

'What he means, Cora, is that air crews are so darned boring to most normal folk, we're the only ones who can stand one another's company,' said Tony.

'Speak for yourself, young Cullen.' The captain winked at her.

'This is a very different lifestyle for me,' she said. 'On the phone to my mother, I mentioned my Rotterdam flight and she sounded quite taken aback. Asked how long we were staying.'

Bing nodded. 'To us, it becomes just another day at the office. To others, the idea of shuttling back and forth between the UK and the continent is startling.'

'Someone has to do it,' said Tony. He smiled at Cora. 'So how did it go? Bing said he found a haven of peace when he went back to chat with people.'

'Hardly peaceful with those engines! But I loved it,' said Cora. 'Once I got over the shock of realising I was on my own.'

'She loved it.' Tony shook his head dolefully as they reached the flying club. 'That'll soon fade.'

But Cora wasn't sure she agreed. The flying bug had bitten her hard and she wasn't complaining.

The return flight proved uneventful. Back at Bristol, Bing announced he was taking his wife to the coast for the weekend, as he wasn't due to fly again until Monday.

'Do you fancy a bite to eat, Cora?' Tony stood back to allow Captain Crosby to leave the DC3.

'That'd be lovely,' she said. 'I'm just finishing up here.'

'I'll see you in the office then.'

She made sure she'd left everything tidy, picked up her possessions and before leaving, realised those training days in the Beehive already seemed light-years away. Days would soon turn into weeks, helping her confidence increase.

*   *   *

With the summer schedules underway, Cora read her weekly roster and saw her name next to Wendy's for a charter trip the following weekend.

On the Saturday morning her bus

arrived at the airport stop a few minutes later than normal, causing her to hurtle towards the terminal building as if pursued by devils. She wrenched open the office door, almost colliding with someone hurrying out.

'Hey, where's the fire?'

'I'm so sorry,' stammered an embarrassed Cora. She met the other person's eyes. 'Oh, it's you!'

Ross Anderson stood, holding the door wide. 'Afraid so. My mind was elsewhere so it must be my fault. Are you all right?'

'Of course.' If you didn't count the bumping heartbeat, the tortuous tummy trembling and sudden drying of her mouth, she supposed she was fine.

Ross grinned. 'I might've known we'd collide again at some point.' He looked over her shoulder. 'Ah, here's Miss Baker. Do come through. Cora and I have finished apologising to each other now.'

'Why do I get a feeling of déjà vu? Hello, you two,' said Wendy.

'I'll see you both on board,' said Ross, heading off.

'Did you know he was flying today?' Wendy asked as they went into the office. 'Is this a one-off?'

'I've no idea,' said Cora. 'I don't even know who our captain is.'

'Nor me.'

'George Tracey,' the station manager called. 'Complete with white silk scarf and handlebar moustache. You'll love him.' He reached for his ever-present mug of tea. 'And ladies, your champagne, ice cubes, silver bucket and finest crystal goblets are already on board.'

'Plastic glasses more like,' said Wendy. 'Aren't we supposed to serve snacks?'

'All under control. Open sandwiches and deliciously sticky pastries — strictly passengers only, remember. Don't let that blue-eyed boy wangle any, whatever you do!' Cora and Wendy exchanged glances.

When the girls walked out onto the tarmac, Ross was carrying out his checks, his attention focused on the aircraft.

'I wonder if he's got the Bristol posting,' said Wendy.

'If he has, he'll probably request an immediate transfer, on the grounds that Air Hostess Murray poses a definite danger.'

The remark, although light-hearted, inspired one of Wendy's searching looks. 'In more ways than one, if you ask me,' she said.

'Come on.' Cora quickened her steps. 'Why don't you be number one for the outbound trip? We'll change over on the return.'

The girls worked well together. Cora found herself wishing they could be crewed together more often but this, being a VIP flight, required two hostesses simply to ensure superior service. Flying over England's patch-work quilt of fields, they served coffee and biscuits. They poured glasses of chilled bubbly high above cottonwool clouds, offering nibbles to keep the passengers from becoming peckish and, as Wendy said, to help soak up the sparkling wine.

On arrival at Reims, their passengers disembarked and were whisked off in a coach. The two hostesses completed their tasks and met up with the pilots.

'Taxi into town, I think,' said Captain Tracey. 'We're booked at the Grand so we should be comfortable. Anyone else stayed there before?'

'This is our first visit,' said Cora.

'Ah, well you should go and look at the cathedral,' he said. 'It's not far from our hotel.'

Ross was looking around. 'Where's Jock got to? He said he wouldn't be long.'

'He's like a hen fussing over a chick, with that aircraft,' said George, fingering his moustache. 'Dedicated is not the word.'

'Are all flight engineers called Jock?' Cora looked from George to Ross. 'I've only ever met two and each one's known as Jock.'

George chuckled. 'It happens,' he said. 'Don't worry your pretty head over it. Here's Flight Engineer Marshall now. Let's find a taxi.'

'Does he have to sound quite so patronising?' Cora muttered to Wendy.

'It's just his way,' said Wendy. 'Everyone says he's very traditional, very protective of his cabin crew. Take no notice.'

'Hmm.' Cora wasn't so sure about that, but soon they all five piled into a cab and headed towards the city.

'I'm ravenous,' announced Ross. 'I was hoping there'd be leftovers.'

'Hard luck, Ross. The champagne must have sharpened that crowd's appetites,' said Wendy.

'They probably wanted to keep their strength up,' said George Tracey. 'I'm told they're including as many visits to champagne producers as they possibly can.'

'They'll probably all have hangovers tomorrow on the flight home,' said Cora.

'Hooray! Let us know if they can't face their food,' said Ross.

'Some of us have to watch our waistlines,' said Cora primly.

The three men looked at one another. 'This,' said Jock Marshall, 'is one of those occasions when it's very difficult to find the right thing to say.'

'You should know,' said Ross. 'Haven't you been married for centuries?'

'And loving every wee second,' sighed Jock, grey eyes twinkling.

'What I'd like to know is how long we get for sightseeing,' said Wendy.

'You're free for the rest of the day, my dear,' said George. 'Tomorrow we'll need to gather in the foyer no later than fourteen hundred hours, ready to go to the airport.'

Cora was still adjusting to using the 24-hour clock but could manage to subtract 12 from 14.

'I'm sure we'll cram in lots of things,' said Wendy.

'Reims is a favourite place of mine,' said George. 'But my wife and I have friends living close by so they're collecting me later. I'm sure Ross and Jock will look after you.'

Cora bit her lip. She'd been about to say something along the lines of she and Wendy being capable of finding their own way around. But she thought better of it, rapidly learning how the dynamics of a crew could differ.

'Me?' Jock chuckled. 'Sorry, you two, but I'm in dire need of a kip.'

* * *

The Grand Hotel loomed in grey stone magnificence as their driver pulled up outside. Cora peered up at the narrow windows with their carved wooden shutters and admired the ornate stone steps sweeping up to the swing doors. Inside the foyer, they walked across a marble floor. Oil paintings were hung on the dark panelled walls. When she and Wendy were shown their second floor room, everything looked clean and inviting.

Wendy bounced on the bed nearest the window. 'This is the life,' she said. 'Let's get changed, then find Jock and Ross. What was the name of that bistro again?'

'Bistro Flo.'

'Flo's Bistro?' Wendy roared with laughter. 'That doesn't sound very French.'

'They said the food's out of this world.' Cora hesitated. 'I'm not sure I want to wander around with too many people after lunch.' She unzipped her overnight bag so fiercely, her friend jumped.

'Well, given Captain Tracey's buzzing off with his friends and Jock's desperate to catch up on his sleep, that only leaves Ross, you and me.'

'Precisely,' said Cora.

'Are you saying you want to be left alone with First Officer Anderson?'

8

Cora felt a pang of guilt, seeing the surprise and disappointment in Wendy's hazel eyes. She pulled a woollen sweater from her case and shook it. 'Heavens above, no, of course not!'

'Pretty colour,' said Wendy. 'Pink makes me look like a demented strawberry. So, what's your problem?'

'I just don't think Ross and I get on that well. Nothing specific.'

'You could've fooled me. Your paths keep crossing, but that's how it is with aviation. You mightn't see someone for ages then keep bumping into them down the route.'

'I . . . I suppose so.' Cora hung up the sweater and shook out a lime-green coatdress.

Wendy was changing into a vivid blue jersey wool top and skirt. 'We'll have lunch,' she said. 'Decide where we go afterwards. If the two chaps want to do something different, that's up to them. But you and I stick together. Right?'

'You bet,' said Cora, arranging her uniform neatly on hangers. 'Let's change some money into francs at the desk. I need to buy something nice for Mum's birthday.'

'Frilly underwear? Chic gloves?'

'She's more of an aertex kind of person,' said Cora. 'But I'm sure she'd like French leather gloves or posh soap.'

★　★　★

'You're in the right place if you're looking for gifts,' said Jock as the four enjoyed savoury omelettes in the delightful bistro. 'Chocolates are always a good bet.'

'I might buy the gift first, then take it back to the hotel before we visit the cathedral. Would that suit you, Wendy?'

'Fine by me.' She looked at Ross. 'Do you have plans, or do you want to come with us?'

Cora held her breath, wishing to be near enough to kick Wendy's ankle.

'It's a nice offer but I think I'll wander round the town, probably end up in the cathedral. Take some photographs. Last time I was here, there wasn't time to see much.'

'Do you folks fancy meeting up for dinner?' Jock asked.

'Will you be awake by then?' Cora teased.

'Never let it be said I'd ever risk missing my dinner, bonnie lass! This ham's very moreish, isn't it?'

'It's a speciality of the region,' said Ross. 'Along with a few cheeses and the *boudin blanc*.'

'What was that last one?' Wendy leaned forward.

'A kind of white pudding,' said Cora. 'Definitely an acquired taste.'

'Now black pudding's a different matter entirely.' Jock shook his head in wonderment. 'I don't want to think about what goes into a white one.'

'Shall we meet in the foyer at seven?'

Ross changed the subject. 'Nods all around? Good. How about coffee now?'

'Yes, please,' said Cora. Why did he have to wear a blue shirt so perfectly matching the colour of his eyes? It just wasn't fair on a girl. In uniform, First Officer Anderson might have stepped straight off the cover of a romantic novel, with his peaked cap perched jauntily on his golden head. In casual clothes, she thought he looked even better. Her gaze lingered on him a little longer than she'd intended and when he turned back again, having caught the waiter's attention, his blue eyes focused straight on her. For moments she felt she soared high above the busy café with its buzz of conversation and scrumptious smells.

To her horror, hastily removing her gaze to focus on the newly arrived coffee pot, she noticed Jock nudge Wendy none too discreetly.

Ross rubbed his hands together. 'I'll pour,' he said. 'Can't have our hostesses complaining about having to wait upon us when they're off duty.'

'I'm impressed,' said Wendy. 'Bet you wouldn't do such a thing if Captain Tracey was here.'

Everyone chuckled. Everyone understood George's opinion about women's roles. The moment passed but Cora knew something bothered Ross. The electricity sparking between the two of them had no business crackling like that. Ross was a man planning marriage and even though his fiancée lived in France, his heart surely belonged to her.

Cora sipped her coffee while the other three discussed French films they'd seen. She felt relieved when Wendy drained her cup and suggested making a move.

Outside, the two strolled along the pavements until they found a chocolate shop whose enticing window display would tempt a saint.

'Just look!' Wendy grabbed Cora's arm. 'Those are amazing. But you daren't buy them if your mum doesn't have all her own teeth!'

'She has, thank goodness.' Cora followed Wendy's pointing finger. The foil-wrapped bonbons, each one the size of a ping-pong ball, were piled upon a silver cake stand.

'Listen to this. They contain hazelnuts, pistachios, marzipan and brandy all wrapped in dark chocolate,' said Cora, peering at the description. 'I knew my French would come in handy one day.'

'Well, take note of this shop, but it's never a good thing to dive into the first that takes our eye, is it?'

'Not when the one next door sells so many gorgeous things.' It was Cora's turn to grab her friend's arm. 'Look at that scarf. It'd be perfect for you, Wendy. You suit that misty shade of green.'

'Let me calculate.' Wendy inspected the price ticket. 'Is that their funny way of writing a seven? Please let it be a figure one.'

'Unfortunately it's a continental

seven. But it's still not expensive, considering it's so beautiful.'

'Let's go on a bit further,' said Wendy. 'We've hardly walked any distance.'

'I wasn't aiming to go for a hike after the hectic morning we had.'

'Good point. How about some gentle window-shopping, then a sit down with a cool drink at one of those pavement cafés? You wouldn't think it was only April, would you?'

'And we're not that much further south,' said Cora. 'I'm not complaining though. This is great.'

'I wonder how many more charter flights we'll do over the next months.'

'According to Tony, the summer's very busy with the scheduled routes anyway,' said Cora.

'Imagine flying out of Gatwick on the Elizabethan. I'd love to see Athens and Rhodes,' said Wendy wistfully.

'Itchy feet already?' Cora teased.

They stopped to peer into a perfumer's window. Every possible shape and size bottle and flask was scattered on pools of velvet and satin. Silk magnolias and strings of shiny pearls gleamed amongst the display.

'Two minds with but a single thought,' said Wendy, pushing open the door.

'Yes, I'd love to try some of these scents.'

'Well, now's your chance to show off your French.'

An attractive young saleswoman glided forward. She wore her raven's wing black hair in a chignon and boasted a complexion as smooth and faultless as the pearls in the window.

'It is OK.' She smiled at them. 'I speak English, *mesdemoiselles*, but I'm happy if you wish to speak in French.'

'My friend will enjoy that.' Wendy beamed. 'I'd love to try Shalimar.'

'Of course.' The assistant shimmied towards a row of miniature glass sprays. 'A little on your wrist, *mademoiselle*?'

Wendy allowed the gentle mist to settle, then sniffed her skin. 'It's divine,' she said, holding out her arm to Cora.

'Do you know the story behind the scent?' the salesgirl asked.

'No.' Wendy raised her eyebrows at Cora. 'We'd love to hear it.'

'Well,' said the assistant. 'Around four centuries ago in Northern India, there was a young man who became dazzled by the beauty of a young woman. From then onwards, his one aim was to make her life a perpetual garden of delights.' She paused.

'How romantic,' Wendy said. 'Lucky girl, whoever she was.'

'From the earth sprang the Gardens of Shalimar. Many years later, this story of enduring love fired the imagination of Monsieur Jacques Guerlain, and in 1925 he created the world's first oriental fragrance.'

Wendy brought her wrist back to her nose. 'It's sublime.'

'It is a blend of flowers and amber and something I believe to be quite woody — a subtle mix, don't you think?'

'It's wonderful but maybe a little expensive for me.'

The assistant nodded. 'I shall give you each a tiny sample. No other perfume can rival this as the essence of love and femininity.'

* * *

'That lily-of-the-valley soap I bought for Mum smells wonderful. And I think we should stock Shalimar on board,' said Cora as they left the hotel again.

'I'm on the Rotterdam flight next Tuesday,' said Wendy. 'I could order a few small bottles from the stores.' She whistled. 'A little goes a long way though.'

'I found Helen's perfume quite overwhelming when I flew with her,' said Cora.

'I know what you mean,' said Wendy. 'Especially when you haven't long had your cornflakes. But Shalimar isn't one to wear for work, I fancy. You'd need to be wearing an elegant dress or a slinky evening gown. You're the expert on that.'

'It seems ages since my gown store days,' said Cora.

They stopped to gaze up at Reims Cathedral.

'I read about it in my father's guidebook last night,' said Wendy.

Cora shot her an amused glance. 'So you can answer all my questions?'

'I'm hopeless at remembering dates but I know all the French kings were crowned here. It's France's equivalent of Westminster Abbey.'

'It's an amazing building.' Cora pointed. 'That rose window's too exquisite for words.'

'There's a gargoyle that reminds me of Captain Tracey,' said Wendy, pointing also.

Cora peered upwards. 'I shouldn't laugh, but I can see what you mean.'

'Let's go inside,' said Wendy. 'There's too much history attached to this place to try and remember it all.'

'There'll be lots of galleries and

stained glass,' said Cora. 'Come on then.' She followed Wendy inside, escaping the sounds of a city Saturday afternoon and marvelling at the building's sheer height and splendour. Goodness only knew how long it took to create. The carvings, the statues, every curve and every column contributed to its dignity.

She heard a babble of languages spoken as they joined others gazing upward and pointing at artefacts. Some sat quietly, meditating or praying or simply soaking up the atmosphere. Cora lost track of time.

'If it's still sunny outside, shall we find a pavement café?' Wendy appeared beside her.

'Why not?'

'You were miles away. I'm sorry to butt in.'

'I felt overcome by it all.'

'I know. It's a little different from life with Castle Airways, isn't it?' Wendy led the way back.

'The cathedral's so timeless, so

ancient, it makes me feel humble. I'm probably talking a load of rubbish here,' Cora said.

'No, you're not. It's exactly what I meant.'

'We rush around so much nowadays,' said Cora.

'You're lucky you're not flying on jets.'

'I'm quite happy with our dear old Dakota, thanks. It's quite speedy enough for me.' Cora chuckled. 'I doubt I'm high-powered enough for a big international airline like BOAC.'

'Mmm,' said Wendy. 'You might get a surprise if you tried.'

Cora shook her head as they left. 'Not for me. I get the distinct impression you'd like to spread your wings though.'

Wendy groaned. 'That's an awful pun. I'm still a new girl, remember.'

'We both are.'

'The awful thing is, I feel as if the more flights I do, the more places I want to see.'

'Well you'll just have to be patient, won't you? Apply for a Gatwick posting next year.'

'I sound ungrateful, don't I? My mother keeps telling me I should settle down and count my blessings.'

'Mothers have to say things like that,' said Cora. 'That's what they're there for.'

'Ha! Shall we try that place?' Wendy pointed towards a café, its pavement tables shaded by green and white striped parasols.

'That'll do. I don't think my feet will ever be the same. Whoops, watch out!' Cora pulled her friend from the path of a cyclist practising for the Tour de France.

'Try not to get killed,' said an amused masculine voice.

Cora whirled round to find herself face to face with Ross.

'Thank goodness Cora's tuned in to the traffic,' said Wendy. 'Phew. Why do they have to drive on the wrong side?'

'How about I buy you both a drink?'

'That'd be lovely,' said Cora, determined to keep hold of her emotions. 'We wondered about that café across the way.'

'I was about to go into the cathedral but decided to leave it until tomorrow,' said Ross.

'Won't they be holding Sunday services?' Wendy asked.

'All the better. I can hide in a corner. I'm not fond of tourists.'

'Dear me,' Cora chided him. 'Where would the airline be without tourists needing to be transported, First Officer?'

'Sorry,' said Ross. 'You know what I mean, though.'

'You're apologising again.'

This time when he fixed her with that blue-eyed gaze, she didn't look away. Wendy hid a smile and made no comment.

But once Ross had walked them back to their hotel and the two girls were alone in their room, Wendy posed a question that her friend couldn't answer. But whether or not the charming first officer had a dark side, Cora knew, despite his flirtatious manner, she had no intention of becoming romantically entangled with him.

Ross opted to keep walking after leaving the two air hostesses. He needed to scold himself because the way he reacted to Cora's nearness didn't fit his master plan. Flying topped his agenda and he wouldn't rest until he claimed those important four gold rings.

Deep within, Ross realised he lived a lie by clinging to the existence of a French fiancée. Surely something weak existed in his character if he needed to hide behind Nicole? He always had ready a little dossier of facts, in case of questions, and of course his mind's eye retained her image. Now, time after time, another more vivid image blocked Nicole's. His cheeks burned with shame as he imagined the disbelief in Cora's eyes should she ever discover his pathetic secret.

He'd reached the canal bank. Remembering his promise to meet the flight engineer before dinner, Ross sighed and stalked back the way he'd come.

9

After their evening meal, Jock suggested seeing a film.

'Whatever's showing,' he said, 'it'll be a change for us.'

'Hang on, French is double Dutch to me,' said Wendy.

'If it's an American or British film, we'll be all right,' said Cora.

'Count me out,' said Ross. 'I'm going to find a little café and sit and watch the world go by.'

'That sounds tempting,' said Jock. 'But I fancy a film.'

'Tell you what,' said Ross. 'I'll come with you and check they're showing something you'd all like to see. If not, we'll reconsider our tactics.'

Jock reckoned he knew the way and soon they stood outside the movie theatre. He pointed. 'Yippee, it's *Goldfinger*. I haven't seen it.'

'James Bond's fine by me,' said Wendy.

Cora hesitated. 'I've seen it already. It's great, but I really don't want to sit through it again.' She read the show times. 'Sorry, but you need to get tickets now if you don't want to miss the beginning.'

Jock grabbed Wendy's hand. 'Come on. See you later, you two.'

Wendy called over her shoulder, 'Make sure someone gives you and me a wake-up call tomorrow, Cora. Just in case!'

Cora chuckled as Jock and Wendy vanished inside. 'We each have a travel alarm but I'd better do as I'm told,' she said.

'I'm sorry if your evening isn't turning out how you'd imagined it would.' Ross turned to her, eyes concerned.

'You don't need to apologise, nor do you have to baby-sit me, First Officer Anderson.' She looked into the distance, determined not to drown in

148

those sparkling blue eyes.

'I realise that,' he said. 'But I'd appreciate your company if you can put up with mine.'

They walked on in silence, Cora's mind contemplating some of the questions she longed to ask. But what gave her the right to interrogate him? Wendy's curiosity was no reason to demand Ross reveal his life story over a cup of coffee simply because they happened to be stranded together for a few hours.

The breeze whipped Cora's hair across her face and she pulled the collar of her jacket up as they walked along.

Ross glanced at her. 'It's too chilly to sit outside. How about we try the café around the corner from the hotel? It looks OK. Are you game?'

He led the way and within minutes they were seated at a corner table. Logs burned in a vast stone fireplace set in oak-panelled walls, with gilt-framed mirrors and gleaming brass everywhere. Ross ordered hot chocolate for Cora and coffee with Calvados for himself.

'Apple brandy,' he explained as the waiter hurried away. 'It's a speciality of Normandy, rather strong, so I wouldn't be drinking it if we were flying first thing tomorrow.'

Maggie Martin had dinned into her trainees the perils of drinking on duty or within twelve hours of a flight. The chief hostess's voice echoed in Cora's head. As for the pilots, they risked reputation and livelihood by ignoring the rules.

A candle in a bottle dripping with melted wax trails stood next to a white triangular ashtray. Edith Piaf's poignant song, '*Je ne Regrette Rien*', played softly in the background.

'I wonder how many people can say the same,' said Ross.

'Pardon? Oh, you mean about having no regrets. Surely you're much too young to be thinking like that?'

He shrugged. A lock of fair hair tumbled across his forehead but he took no notice. After a moment he said, 'I think my mother would prefer me to have become a scientist or a doctor rather than a pilot. But I knew I'd never settle until at least starting to train and test my aptitude. So that's one regret I don't have.'

'Is your mother resigned to your choice now?' Cora asked.

'Hard to say.' He sat back as their drinks arrived.

'Has she ever been on board one of your flights?'

His face brightened. 'Not with Castle. But I've taken her up a couple of times in one of our local flying club's aircraft.'

'Did she enjoy that?' Cora looked down appreciatively at her tall glass of steaming hot chocolate.

'Apparently.' He sipped his drink and winced. 'First swallow's always a shock. Then you get a kind of glow.'

'Sounds fun,' she said.

Ross laughed and leaned forward, elbows on the table. 'I don't make a habit of drinking this stuff, in case you're wondering.'

'It's a bit wasted on me,' she said. 'Being in the heart of the champagne region, I mean.'

'Maybe you'd like a small liqueur when you've finished your hot chocolate. Benedictine is sweeter than Calvados. More mellow. I guarantee you won't feel drunk.'

'We'll see,' said Cora. 'This is great, being here. I'd have happily watched a film I hadn't already seen, but I'd far rather soak up the atmosphere.'

'Making the most of an opportunity?' His voice was a murmur.

She stirred her drink. Ross stretched out a hand and closed it around hers as she replaced the spoon. 'Please don't,' she said.

'Don't what? Deny the attraction I feel for you?'

'I'm probably a novelty,' she muttered.

'You're wrong. I'm afraid your warning's come too late. I've been fighting this but without success.'

Cora knew she should withdraw her

hand, but something in his eyes prevented her. 'Maybe I'd better have that liqueur after all.' Her voice sounded calmer than she felt. Wendy's question had voiced Cora's own thoughts and it needed to be answered, for all their sakes.

Ross loosed his clasp on her fingers. Pushed back that floppy cowlick with a boyish gesture. Nodded to a hovering waiter. 'A glass of Benedictine for the lady, please,' he said, speaking in French.

'I'm impressed,' Cora said.

'Ordering food and drink is about as far as it goes,' he said. 'Probably that didn't help matters.'

She sipped more hot chocolate, wondering what he meant. Wondering where this was going, afraid to find out, yet afraid to spoil the moment. But what kind of hussy did he think she was? She'd no intention of allowing this handsome young pilot to two-time his fiancée with her. They sat in silence until the liqueur arrived.

Ross raised his brandy balloon. '*Santé,*' he said. 'That really is the limit of my French.'

Cora chinked glasses with him. 'Now we've toasted each other's health, don't you think you should explain?'

'Yes.'

Cora watched his jaw tighten, the contours of his face etched sharply in the candlelight. Impatiently, she urged him on. 'You're not making any kind of sense, Ross. What concerns me is how you can speak so . . . so wildly about attraction when you already have a fiancée.' She sipped her liqueur, relishing its sweet herby warmth.

She saw his face contort. Still he hesitated.

'How come you didn't catch a train to Paris after we checked in? You'd have had plenty of time to visit Nicole before we go back tomorrow. I'd better tell you, it's not only me wondering what you're playing at.'

'I'm well aware how aircrew love to gossip.' He took a deep breath. 'OK. To be honest, there is no Nicole,' he said. 'Or, should I say, my former fiancée once was but is no longer part of my life.'

Cora stopped hearing the background buzz, the clattering crockery and the caramel voice of the French crooner who'd replaced Edith Piaf's plaintive song. Nor did she see anything except for the man seated opposite, cradling a glass in his hands. Well-groomed hands, she noticed, finding this reassuring. In those hands, Ross needed to hold the lives of thousands of passengers, not to mention fellow crew members.

'What must you think of me?'

She met his gaze. 'Try me.'

'I'll explain everything, I promise, but I want you to know I'm not fighting off hordes of girls. I'm not a Don Juan; please don't think of me as such.'

She shook her head, still bewildered. 'Why would you be besieged by girls when everyone thinks you're engaged?'

'Exactly,' said Ross. 'I proposed to

Nicole just over a year ago. It was far too hasty, as I soon discovered. I think she thought it glamorous having a pilot for a boyfriend.'

'How did you two meet?'

'I was in London, walking through Hyde Park one day, and I sat down on a bench, killing time before an appointment. I didn't notice her until the man sitting between us finished his sandwiches and left. Nicole was sightseeing with friends and had wandered away on her own. She looked up from her map, saw me and thought I should be able to find the place she needed to get to.'

'You were in uniform?'

'Oh, yes. As I said, I was young. I was just as dazzled by this attractive Frenchwoman, almost through training to be a doctor, as she was by the idea of going out with a pilot. Looking back, the whole thing was farcical.'

'Yet you proposed marriage?'

'I was totally infatuated. She spoke almost perfect English; she was bright, bubbly, fun to be with; and somehow, a couple of months later, after a delicious dinner in a little restaurant overlooking the Seine, I asked her to marry me.'

'So it was a moonlight and brandy moment?' Cora kept on twisting her fingers together.

'Something like that,' he said. 'We went out next morning and chose a ring. At that time I was flying for a small airfreight company but I'd already applied to Castle. They granted me an interview and once I joined them, I hardly ever got to Paris.'

'Didn't she travel to London to see you?'

'Only once. To be fair she was bogged down with her medical studies.' Cora waited.

'Absence doesn't always make the heart grow fonder. In any case, she wanted to work in Paris after qualifying and there was no way I could be based in France, not if I stayed with Castle.'

'I'm sorry,' said Cora.

'Don't be. The whole thing was

157

disastrous, rather like a hastily made soufflé flopping like a pancake once it left the oven.'

So he was unattached. Cora's hand trembled as she raised her glass. 'So why does everyone believe you're still engaged?'

'This is the embarrassing part. I decided life would be a lot easier if I wasn't perceived as an eligible young pilot.' He raised his chin. 'Now do you see what I mean when I say that makes me sound big-headed? As if I consider myself to be God's gift to women?'

'What's the real reason, Ross?'

He stared back at her. Swallowed hard. 'It didn't take you long to figure that out, did it?'

'You're certainly not arrogant and conceited. You enjoy female company. So there has to be something else. You don't have to tell me but you might find it helps if you do.' She hesitated. 'I know how difficult it can be to make wise judgements about people. I haven't known you long but I'm not about to broadcast your private life to all and sundry.'

He wound his fingers around the stem of his brandy goblet. Cora took another sip of her drink. Again she felt the warm, rich glow of the liqueur travel through her. Sweet. Intoxicating. Dangerous.

'Thank you,' he said. 'But be warned. I'll probably sound as if I'm in the psychiatrist's chair.'

'Don't worry about how you sound. I hate the thought of you bottling all this up.' She didn't add, how like a man it was to cocoon his innermost feelings in a web of secrecy.

She listened as it all came rushing out. How, as a three-year-old when his dad was shot down, he still had this impression of his mum in floods of tears. Ross remembered scrambling into her lap and feeling her wet cheeks as he pressed his face close. Still recalled how she'd rocked him in her arms at bedtime, as if she couldn't bear to let him go.

'Later on, I knew I wanted to follow in my father's footsteps and make a career from flying. My mother wanted me to go to university, so I chose an engineering course. I wasn't sure about joining the RAF, so the alternative was air training college.'

'It goes without saying, you loved flying,' said Cora, watching his face glow.

'I was lucky to gain a place and I lived for it. But the desire to build on my first successes grew and grew like a fire consuming me.' He smiled. 'It was as if I wanted to do what I think my father would have done, had he survived the war.'

'Your dad would've been another Captain Tracey by now,' said Cora. 'Someone who learnt to fly in the RAF, then become a WW2 fighter pilot on the Lancaster or whatever?'

Ross nodded slowly. 'It was as if I was taking over from him. I became — have become — very single-minded. I'm afraid I'm a very boring person and

160

one who shelters behind a lie, in order to achieve a dream.'

Cora watched him signal to the waiter and bit her lip, wondering whether to comment.

'Don't worry,' he said. 'This will be my last one. I don't normally bother much with alcohol.'

'Is it me who's driving you to drink? I do hope not!'

Ross laughed. 'Not at all. It's because I'm so relaxed, sitting here talking to you, that I can let myself unwind. You've no idea what a relief it is to share this. I feel as if a big black cloud has lifted.'

Their waiter took an order for another Calvados and a hot chocolate and sped away.

'I meant it when I said I wouldn't tell anyone about our conversation,' said Cora. 'But now you've broken the silence, don't you think you should make your new status known?'

'Oh dear. I really can't see myself confessing to all those people,' he said.

'Surely all you have to do is tell one or two and let them do the rest?'

'Hmm. I suppose you do have a point. Captain Tracey may be capable of landing on a sixpence but he's a real old woman when it comes to a bit of juicy gossip.'

Cora chuckled. 'I'll bear that in mind.'

'Here's our waiter.' They sat back as their drinks were placed before them.

'I imagine your mother and stepfather know about your broken engagement?' Cora asked once they were alone again.

'Yes. I told them not long afterwards. Mother only met Nicole once but she said she liked her. She seemed to take the news of our break-up in her stride though.'

'What about your stepfather?'

'He's a nice fellow. Knows nothing about flying but he teaches Mathematics. My mother met him at some sort of charity do.'

'If your family know, don't you think

162

your closest friends should be told next? What if you come clean to the crew this weekend and Tony finds out in a few days' time and feels slighted because you haven't confided in him?'

Ross bit his lip. 'You're right of course. I'll keep quiet 'til I see old Cullen and another chum of mine, who's based in Manchester. I'll give Tony a bell soon or stick a note in his pigeonhole.'

'So you're still waiting to hear about a posting?'

'I'm due in Gatwick on Monday for a chat with the chief pilot. Either to learn where my next posting is, or have him tell me to get on my bike.'

'I rather doubt that!' Cora's response was polite but she hadn't anticipated such a sharp twinge of alarm at the thought of Ross quitting the airline.

'I've been stupid, haven't I?' He swirled his glass gently so the golden liquid surged from side to side.

'You've done no harm, that's the main thing. Except possibly break the heart of a hopeful hostess or two.'

'I don't think so. In fact, I'm not really sure why I've kept up this pretence so long. Thank goodness we were crewed together this weekend, Cora.'

It might have been the warmth in his eyes. It might have been the richness of her hot chocolate. But whatever it was, she felt as though she floated on a fluffy pink cloud. And that wouldn't do, whether First Officer Ross Anderson was unattached or not. She, too, had a career to think of, and she loved her new life.

He placed his elbows on the table, propped up his chin and bent forward. Cora watched him reposition the candle before reaching to take her hands in his.

'Some time I'd like us to go out for dinner, just you and me. If you'd allow it, that is.'

'That's kind, but there's really no need.' She hoped the candlelight would disguise her unease. 'Besides, we probably won't be crewed together again for ages.'

He frowned. 'Does that mean you won't contemplate coming out with me? Unless we happen to be flying together?'

'That's not what I meant at all,' she said patiently. 'I meant I didn't want you to think you must treat me to a meal in exchange for my having listened to you.'

'Air Hostess Murray,' he said. 'I'm asking you for a date. When and where, for obvious reasons I cannot yet say. You've made me see the error of my ways and I don't want to end up a sad old loner.'

'I wouldn't want to be accused of distracting you from your career,' she said, unable to hide a smile.

'Ouch! I deserved that. So, will you accept my open-ended invitation? Please?' He squeezed her hands gently.

Suddenly she wanted him to kiss her. The tenderness in his eyes and the feel of her fingers being trapped oh so comfortably in his much larger hands made her feel as if she was wrapped in sunshine. By helping him talk through his reasons for keeping up that silly pretence, she'd shattered his defences. But did this mean Ross was ready to risk becoming emotionally involved? If so, how did she feel about that?

Cora told herself not to be stupid. He was waiting for an answer to his friendly invitation. Friendly. That was the word! As in platonic friendship.

She nodded. 'I'm happy to go out for a meal some time. 'It's hard to keep in touch with friends, working the hours we do.'

It was his turn to nod. Slowly. 'Indeed. Is that how you see me?'

Deliberately she misunderstood. 'Of course. I like to think we've begun a nice friendship this weekend. Now we've stopped apologising to one another,' she added slyly.

He released her hands. 'Maybe you'll let me have your phone number tomorrow. As soon as I know my schedule, I'll get in touch.'

'If I'm out, you can leave a message

with my landlord,' she said. 'Or with whichever tenant happens to pick up the phone.'

He nodded. 'Would you rather I rang your home number and left a message?'

'No,' said Cora quickly. Her mother was the last person she wanted interfering in her social life. She loved her mum, but Arlene's insistence that Dave was Cora's Mr Right frankly got right up her nose! 'I don't ring them that often,' she added. 'I love them dearly but you know how it is with parents.' Immediately, she regretted her tactless remark.

Ross didn't seem to notice her faux pas. 'I'm sure you're a loving daughter,' he said. 'Now, I'd better walk you back to the hotel, then I think I'll take one more stroll before heading to my room.' He stood up.

'Pilot's paunch threatening?' Cora rose too.

'Don't be cheeky.' He gave their waiter a wave and indicated the francs he'd left to pay the tab, before helping

Cora into her jacket.

As she stepped out into the late evening chill, Cora shivered. Ross moved closer, placing a protective arm around her. Then he gently cupped her chin. 'Look at those stars.'

Obediently she gazed upwards, making it easy for him to bend his head and brush her lips with his.

'Oh,' she said, not drawing away.

Ross kissed her again, this time with more meaning. And as Jock and Wendy turned the corner, chatting animatedly, they came upon an unexpected but most interesting scenario.

10

'It's so out of character, Cora.' In their room, Wendy tossed her copper curls, turned her back and reached for her pyjamas.

'It was just one of those things,' said Cora, perching on her bed. She was already in her nightdress, having muttered apologies and grabbed their room key while the other three arranged what time to meet for breakfast. How embarrassing had that been, caught kissing someone else's fiancé? Because she'd advised Ross not to tell people his news until he'd informed his best friends, neither of them had been able to do anything but stand there wishing the ground would split and swallow them.

'You don't want to get a reputation,' said Wendy. 'Didn't we agree Ross Anderson was too flirtatious for someone planning marriage?'

'We did,' said Cora. 'Please don't read too much into this. It was just unfortunate you and Jock arrived at that moment.'

'I think it's lucky we did! You might have found yourself in very compromising circumstances.'

'What are you suggesting?' Cora wished her heart wouldn't imitate a piston engine.

'I'm suggesting Ross might have invited you to join him for a nightcap in his room.' Wendy's head disappeared inside the filmy top of her black babydoll pyjamas.

Despite being on the defensive, Cora saw the funny side. There was Wendy acting like a mother superior reprimanding a naughty novice, while Cora, suspected scarlet woman, sat primly on her bed, wearing the winceyette floral nightie her mum gave her when she left for the training course.

'We'd been putting the world to rights. Ross and I have a lot in common, Wendy. Please believe me, I'm not looking for complications. Nor do I want you and me to fall out over a silly misunderstanding.'

'Nor do I. It was a shock seeing you two kissing, but it's really not my business.' Wendy yawned and stretched. 'Do you want to read? I think I'll get my head down.'

'I'll just rub in some hand lotion, then turn the light off.'

'Night-night,' said Wendy. 'Sleep well.'

'Sweet dreams,' said Cora. 'I remembered to book us a morning call.'

When she slithered under the unfamiliar continental quilt, wondering how on earth she'd manage to stay beneath its stodgy puffiness, Cora felt too wide-awake for sleep. Ross had agonised over her reaction to his maintaining the fiancée deception, but she saw nothing too sinister about that. He was a very private person. Cora couldn't help feeling relieved, knowing the attraction between them was no longer shadowed by Nicole's presence.

It still didn't help her come to terms with the existence of that attraction though.

She turned on her other side. Wendy's deep, regular breathing signalled she'd entered the Land of Nod. Dear Wendy — she'd said they should blame the Benedictine for that al fresco kiss.

How sensible would it be to go on a proper date with Ross? Maybe she'd accepted too readily. Maybe fate would intervene, making a meeting impossible. He could be posted anywhere. Her practical side told her, the floodgates having opened, he'd probably extended the invitation off the cuff. He'd been attached to a cardboard girlfriend for a while now and, as Cora had pointed out, he liked female company.

She already enjoyed a platonic relationship with Tony Cullen. Never in a million years would she ever regard Tony as anything but a pal, and she knew deep down he filled the place of the non-existent elder brother she'd longed for as a child.

She might as well face facts. What she felt for Ross was the stuff of romantic novels, so not even a brief, sweet kiss could be allowed from now on. He'd mentioned visiting the cathedral next morning, and breakfast would be a communal affair, with Captain Tracey joining his crew. She'd enjoy a leisurely morning with Wendy and put away any yearnings to lose herself in Ross's embrace again. She hadn't waited all this time to begin a sparkling new life, only to lose not only her heart but also her common sense.

Ross had made his goal in life very clear. If he became diverted, it could cost him. After counting a multitude of fluffy white sheep jumping a towering fence, Cora's mind stopped torturing her, tipping her gently into slumber.

★　★　★

When the planeload of happy passengers disembarked at Bristol on Sunday,

Cora looked forward to a hot bath and early night. She'd be back again next morning, with Bing and Tony, on the usual run — safely away from a certain blue-eyed pilot and the risk of complications.

Captain Tracey had landed his aeroplane at Bristol so silkily, some passengers applauded. He'd touched down minutes ahead of an old friend, a pilot with another airline, who'd flown in from Alicante.

'My old RAF chum and his crew are staying at the same hotel as Ross and me,' Captain Tracey told Wendy and Cora. 'Can I offer you two a lift? We could all have a meal together. What do you reckon, Ross?'

Ross glanced in Cora's direction — something she knew didn't escape Wendy.

'That'd be great,' said Ross. 'But I'm afraid my MGB isn't designed to take more than one normal-size passenger.'

George chortled. 'Well, these two young ladies must spin a coin to see which one accompanies you. There are nine of us, so we'll need a cab as well.'

'Maybe I could ride in the taxi,' Cora said. 'I'm on duty again tomorrow and I really need to get back.'

'I understand,' said George. 'You've done a first-class job this weekend, you two. I'm looking forward to flying with both you young ladies over the summer.'

'I can take you home before going on to the hotel, Cora,' said Ross. 'I'm not setting off tomorrow until after the morning rush.'

Cora hesitated, knowing her refusal would appear churlish.

'Ross, could I just check something in the paperwork with you before we leave?' Flight engineer Jock stood there, scratching his beard, clipboard in hand.

Cora stood behind the Castle Airways check-in desk as crew members drifted towards the main entrance. A man caught her eye when he rose from a chair in the passenger waiting area and at first she thought she was seeing things. But this wasn't the aftermath of two eventful days. She saw someone who hadn't entered her thoughts for several weeks.

'Hello, Cora,' said her former boy-friend. 'I thought I'd come and pick you up. How smart you look in your uniform.'

She froze. Ultra-conservative Dave had caught the fashion bug. He wore a short jacket over a cream polo shirt and dark brown trousers that verged on a flare.

'Dave,' she said. 'I don't know what to say.'

'Ready to go?' Ross appeared in the doorway, immaculate in uniform, three gold rings gleaming on his jacket sleeves.

Cora watched Dave's eyes narrow.

'It's not what you think,' she said.

'What isn't?' Ross looked puzzled.

'I thought I'd surprise Cora,' said Dave. 'But maybe you'd both prefer I went away?'

'Not at all, old chap,' said Ross. 'You

two are obviously friends. I'm sure she's had enough of my company this weekend. You have a lift with your pal, Cora. I'll see you down the route.'

Before she could gather her scattered wits, Ross headed for the main door. She heard him calling to the others. 'Anyone want a lift with me?'

She dragged her attention back to Dave. 'You've come all this way to see me? How did you know what time we'd be landing?'

'I bumped into your mother in town yesterday. She told me you were away in France this weekend. She also gave me your phone number, but by then of course you'd already left. I rang the airport to find out your arrival time.'

Silently, Cora fumed. Her mother had no business handing out her phone number to all and sundry, and particularly not to her ex-boyfriend. Why must everyone try to organise her?

'I think the airport restaurant's still open if your sights are set on supper,' said Dave. 'Would you like that?'

'No, thank you. Look, this is crazy. I wasn't planning to eat with the others. I'm on duty again tomorrow and all I want is a hot bath and my comfortable bed.'

She watched his face fall. 'But I've taken a room in a B and B near your flat. Booked Monday off! Your mother said you normally work alternate days, so how come you're flying again tomorrow?'

Cora watched the door swing shut behind the last crew member. 'I'll explain to you on the way back, now you've taken all this trouble. But only if you understand I really don't want a meal.'

'Could we go somewhere and talk?'

The last thing she intended was to invite him to her place. 'I'm sorry, Dave. Mum had no right to give you her version of how I run my life. You've wasted your time.'

'Ouch,' he said. 'Cora, honey, you must be exhausted. I'm sorry if you feel I've acted thoughtlessly. Let me drive you back. We can have a nice chat on the way. All right?'

She wanted to tell him she wasn't his honey and had no intention of being so but he picked up her overnight bag and strode off. Inwardly fuming, she'd no option but to follow. Her mother was a dear, kind woman but oh, how she wished Arlene would cease fantasising about a daughter dressed in white satin and orange blossom and face the fact that Cora now lived her own dream.

Dave unlocked the passenger door. '*Mademoiselle*'s chariot awaits,' he said.

'How's work going?' Cora asked.

'Promotion's looming. I'll probably be made head of section soon. When I told your mother, she said she always knew I was a golden boy.'

'I'm pleased for you.' Cora's nails bit into her palms.

'That pilot just now,' said Dave, causing Cora's heart to double somersault. 'Has he got his eye on you?'

She waited until he'd joined the main road. 'Could I ask you something?'

'Go ahead.'

'Have you got your eye on any of the women you work with at the council offices?'

'Flipping heck, of course not! One or two are old enough to be my mother.'

'What about the younger ones?'

'What are you getting at, Cora?'

'First Officer Anderson and I were in the same crew this weekend. We're colleagues just like you and your workmates. Contrary to what you imagine, none of us goes around fancying everyone we work with.' She sat upright, gaze fixed on the road ahead.

'Fair enough, but you can't blame me for getting the wrong impression,' said Dave. 'Especially with Captain Marvel standing there, waiting to be admired.'

'That's rubbish,' said Cora. 'For a start, he's a first officer. A pilot wears a uniform because he does a particular job. Ross isn't one bit boastful about his work.' *Unlike you,* she added silently.

She sucked in her breath as an

animal streaked across the road ahead. The car headlights highlighted the creature's bushy tail.

'Mr Fox out looking for supper,' said Dave.

Now, why did that sound so familiar? Cora kept the thought to herself while they crossed the city boundary in silence.

11

'I need to choose a birthday gift for my mother,' said Tony next morning, turning up while Cora checked the cabin.

'Not you as well? I could have brought you something from Reims.'

'Oh yes, how did that go? You were crewed with George Tracey, weren't you? To say nothing of that rascal, Ross.'

Cora stood at the front of the cabin as Tony approached. 'Nice passengers, good company, delicious food and time for sightseeing. Weather conditions excellent for the time of year.' She didn't mention the prevailing emotional conditions.

'Excuse me for saying so, but you don't look your usual sparkling self. Got that Monday morning feeling?' Tony reached for the cockpit door handle.

'My ex boyfriend turned up last night just as I'd accepted a lift from Ross.'

'Ah.' Tony grimaced. 'I have to get on now but if you want to cry on your Uncle Tony's shoulder, why not come with me later and help choose my mother's gift?'

'Emotional blackmail? All right then.'

Another busy Monday meant Cora had her work cut out as tail winds chopped minutes off their flying time. At Liverpool she managed a brief chat with Shirley Plumstead, the darkly glamorous Newcastle-based hostess.

'You'll never guess whose coffee I poured this morning!' Shirley's eyes shone with excitement. 'My mum will be madly jealous when she finds out.'

'Um, Eric Burdon?' said Cora, thinking of the northern pop group.

'Funnily enough, I went to school with him,' said Shirley. 'How about Sean Connery?'

'You're joking! You lucky ducky. So, how does Mr James Bond take his coffee?'

'Stirred not shaken,' said Shirley. 'He was reading a script during the flight but he drank two cups of coffee, thanked me nicely and autographed a serviette for my mother.'

'For you, more like,' teased Cora.

The two headed out to board their respective aircraft.

'We're like yoyos on this route,' said Shirley. 'Spending time at each other's home bases. I love it though, don't you?'

'Yes,' said Cora. 'It's the best job I've ever had and I don't want to stop doing it in the foreseeable future.'

'Is something bothering you, pet? You sound a bit fierce,' said Shirley.

'Sorry. It's just my matchmaking mum.'

'Ah, we've probably all got one of those. They're of an era when to remain unmarried was a stigma. We have different options in our sights nowadays.'

'Like keeping greedy pilots from raiding the biscuit tin?' Cora stopped.

'We're parked over there. Have a good trip, Shirley.'

★   ★   ★

That day was an occasion when the two captains had exchanged car keys so each crew had the use of a vehicle during their off-duty hours up north or down south. Cora sat beside Bing on the way into the city.

'Do you two have anything special planned?' he asked as they travelled through the countryside. 'I want to search the book shops for something I'm after. Shall we have a spot of lunch first?'

'I'm helping Tony do some shopping,' said Cora. 'But I imagine I'm allowed time off for good behaviour.'

'We'll see about that,' said Tony. 'Where had you in mind, Skipper?'

'What about the restaurant at Fenwicks? Would that suit you both?'

'We'll probably shop there,' said Cora. 'It's fine by me.'

'I might fit in a visit to the news cinema afterwards.' Bing shot a sly glance at Cora. 'To function properly, I need my ration of Tom and Jerry.'

'We could always visit the cathedral,' said Tony.

'Ignore him,' said Cora. 'He knows I was sightseeing on Saturday.'

'Reims Cathedral is magnificent,' said Bing. 'Tell me, how was George Tracey? I haven't seen him in a while but I'm sure we'll get together soon.'

Cora sat listening to the pilots' friendly banter while gazing through the window, until the mention of a familiar name grabbed her attention.

'And in the end, I gather the chief pilot decided to give the other Bristol posting to First Officer Anderson,' said Bing.

'Really?' The surprise in Tony's voice told Cora he'd been totally unaware of the news. She wondered if Ross was now arriving at Gatwick to learn his fate while down the route the jungle drums already beat.

'It seems that weekend charter turned out to be a trial run for George and his new first officer,' said Bing.

'It's good news. I must try and meet up with Ross soon,' said Tony. 'There's a plan rumbling around my head and he might like to be involved with it.'

'Well, if you think I can help, let me know,' said Bing. 'At the moment, I'm keeping my eye open for a parking space.'

'My idea has nothing to do with aeroplanes,' said Tony. 'But I'll keep you posted, Skipper.'

★　★　★

After lunch, followed by a quick browse when Tony proved to be a no-nonsense shopper by taking four minutes flat to choose a pretty brooch for his mum, Cora decided she'd done with shops. She joined the pilots for the news cinema visit but her mind wasn't focused upon current affairs.

They took their seats as little Tweety

Pie narrowly escaped the clutches of Sylvester the cat. The strident background chords reminded Cora of the spine-chilling shower scene from Alfred Hitchcock's film *Psycho*. Triumphant music blared as the cute bird hopped out of Sylvester's reach, leaving the furious feline sliding across the kitchen floor, his angelic opponent having tipped over a bottle of cooking oil. This spilled into the moggy's path, allowing the bird to escape.

By contrast, the tragic conflict in Vietnam dominated the news footage. The early budget had slammed four shillings on the cost of a bottle of Scotch and one penny on a pint of beer. Cora, trying not to fidget, wondered whether she dared allow her thoughts to roam where they wanted.

Her mind explored the reality of Ross being based at Bristol. Would Tony and his flatmate make room for him? The two first officers weren't exactly home birds, and while one flew on a Monday the other would be off duty, and vice versa the next day. And what was this idea of Tony's? Would she end up as piggy in the middle, crewed with Tony Cullen, whose cheerful company and friendship she valued but whose best buddy was the young man Cora knew posed a threat to her peace of mind?

And what about your heart? that little inner voice persisted. The night before, after Dave drove her home, he'd told her he hoped she didn't end up lonely, having upped sticks to pursue a fine new career.

'I shouldn't be surprised if this flying lark turns out to be a passing fancy,' he'd said. 'Anyway, your mum told me air hostesses aren't allowed to keep working once they reach 30.' Dave's tone had been dismissive.

'It's 32, actually. With respect, I have quite a few years to go before that landmark.' She'd given a curt thank-you for the lift and banged the car door behind her.

Cora knew Dave was angry with her

for not coming running back to him. She also knew, given the smallest encouragement, he'd like nothing better than to meet her at the airport once or twice a week and take her out somewhere while she was still in uniform. How much keener he appeared, now Cora had left the gown shop to soar above the clouds. Dave's possessive streak had manifested itself like a red flag when Ross had appeared.

Cora fingered the gold pin on her right lapel. She wasn't particularly glamorous, even though people said her uniform suited her. Nor was she convinced she needed a steady boyfriend. With irregular working hours and occasional night stops, sometimes because of challenging weather conditions, personal relationships could soon turn prickly.

Her attention returned to the newsreel. Prime Minister Harold Wilson and President de Gaulle of France had met for talks on Vietnam. To her left, Tony slipped from his seat. By the time he returned, bearing choc ices, the cartoons were on again. Cora prayed she wouldn't drop ice cream down her uniform front.

'I think I'll use my upturned hat as a plate, just in case,' Tony whispered in her ear.

'You're nothing if not resourceful,' she whispered back.

'Good. I like the Road Runner,' said Bing to her right.

Cora subdued an urge to giggle. How fascinating it was, seeing this broad-shouldered wartime fighter pilot fascinated by the scrawny Coyote pursuing Road Runner across the desert.

'Tip-top entertainment,' said Tony.

Mouth full of vanilla ice and dark chocolate, Cora daren't comment.

★　★　★

Back at the airport, Bing and Tony went about their pre-flight routines while

Cora called into the office to check the passenger load.

'Hello, Air Hostess Murray.' A blonde young woman, immaculate in Castle uniform, extended a slim hand. 'It's good to meet you properly.'

The check hostess! Was she merely passing through? That'd be too much to hope. Cora gulped and held out her hand too. 'Good to meet you too, Miss Whitfield. You adjudicated when I sat my exam.'

'That's right. Please call me Jeanne. My parents gave me a French name because they honeymooned in Paris.' Her eyes twinkled. 'But people often call me Jeannie if they've seen it written down so I've given up correcting them.'

'I'll remember,' said Cora, relaxing a little.

'I've no intention of interrupting your routines, but I'll be on your flight this evening. Then returning with Shirley, night-stopping and checking the other hostesses tomorrow.'

'Of course,' said Cora. 'Should I

ignore you? I mean to say, treat you like I'd treat any other passenger,' she added hurriedly.

Jeanne chuckled. 'That sounds just the ticket. I didn't really imagine you ignored your passengers. I'll board ahead of them and tuck myself into a rear seat. You have 15 flying from here.' She paused. 'Everyone's talking about 007 flying with us this morning. That must have made Shirley's day.'

Cora nodded. At least the pressure of knowing she was being scrutinised would allow her no time to think of anything but her duties. She thanked her lucky stars she'd double-checked her uniform jacket and skirt, not to mention her chin, for telltale smudges. The airport wasn't busy and she made her way out to the Dakota, determined to give as crisp a cabin service as possible.

When Tony boarded, she wagged her finger at him. 'You'd better keep Pappa steady this evening, First Officer. Jeanne Whitfield's flying with us —

checking on my cabin service.'

Tony whistled. 'Poor you. They say she's a dragon.'

'Don't make me any more nervous than I already am.'

'Piece of cake,' he said. 'Passing muster with the check hostess, I mean. I heard some interesting information about our Miss Whitfield the other day.' He glanced behind him. 'It'll keep.'

'In my short time with this airline, I've reached the conclusion it runs on gossip, not aviation fuel.'

'And paperwork,' said Tony gloomily. 'Never forget the paperwork.' He made his way up the cabin. 'Day off tomorrow,' he called over his shoulder.

'Unless I'm dismissed on the spot for slovenly service,' murmured Cora, straightening a seatbelt.

'I'll pretend I didn't hear that remark.' He disappeared through the crew door.

But Cora forgot Jeanne's presence, once the first passenger boarded and she fell into her familiar greeting routine. Her pre-flight announcement went without a glitch and the Dakota rumbled towards the runway exactly on schedule. Cora counted heads and informed the captain the passengers were all strapped in.

She made her way to the rear and strapped herself in while the engine noise intensified and the aircraft gave the impression of standing on tiptoe, waiting for the captain to release the brakes.

Soon they were soaring, climbing and distancing themselves from the scattered toy houses and miniature vehicles below. The seatbelt sign remained illuminated and the captain's voice boomed over the public address system. 'Ladies and gentlemen, we anticipate this slight turbulence will last only a few minutes. In the interests of comfort and safety, please keep your seatbelts fastened.'

Cora wondered whether or not she'd be able to offer a drinks service. The businessmen, frequent passengers on this route, sometimes enjoyed a tot of brandy with a cup of coffee. Luckily the seatbelt sign went off before long, and she began work at the galley.

'Thanks.' Last to be served, the check hostess accepted her tray. 'Now perch here a minute, will you?' Jeanne moved her handbag off the adjacent seat. 'Your preparation looked faultless,' she said. 'Your manner with the passengers is delightful. You remembered the names of a few of the regulars and for someone still fairly new to this route, that's excellent. I could hear every word of your announcement. Well done on that. It's not easy competing with the sound of a Dakota's engines.'

'Phew. Thanks, Miss . . . erm, Jeanne.'

'I thought I'd reassure you.' Jeanne sipped her coffee. 'Nice brew.'

When Cora collected the pilots' trays, Tony turned around. 'So you haven't jumped out yet?'

Cora stuck her thumb up. 'She's lovely. You wait till I get you, Tony Cullen.'

'Help,' he said. 'I'm scared.'

'Has he been pulling your leg, Cora? Shall we make him land the goony bird at Liverpool?' Bing gave her a grin.

'And risk frightening the passengers, Captain?' Cora asked.

'Good point,' said Bing.

She left, smiling. It was a rush, collecting and tidying everything away prior to the first officer's smooth-as-silk landing, but she made it in good time. Transit passengers got off to stretch their legs but as the pilots came down the aisle, their faces were less than cheerful.

'Weather's looking grim,' said Bing. 'We'll check again with the met people but be prepared to night-stop here.' They hurried away.

'These things happen,' said Jeanne. 'Let's go inside. And don't look so worried. I imagine the northbound service is on its way but we'll soon find out.'

The ground staff had their work cut out once it was decided Pappa wasn't going anywhere else that night. Fog blanketed the southwest of the UK, but the northbound service had left before the clampdown and would pick up passengers for Newcastle.

While the pilots and ground staff were busy, Jeanne kept Cora entertained, relating mishaps and comical events and every possible mini-drama over the years she'd been flying. 'It can be a right old muddle when the weather plays havoc with schedules,' she said.

'Here's your aircraft just taxiing in,' said Cora, peering through the window.

'Another poor girl to terrify,' said Jeanne. 'You know, I felt exactly the same when my check hostess appeared one morning and announced she was flying to Las Palmas with us.'

'Is she still with the airline?' Cora asked.

'Yes. It was Maggie Martin. Can you imagine? She looked very stern but she was very complimentary, even though I made a complete hash of my announcement.'

'I can't believe that,' said Cora. 'Just think, Maggie went on to become chief air hostess. And so might you, one day.'

'No chance,' said Jeanne. 'Not now I'm expecting.'

Cora froze.

Jeanne's hand flew to her mouth. Eyes wide, she stared at Cora. 'Oh my goodness, I didn't mean to share that information. It just sort of popped out!'

'I . . . I promise not to tell anyone.'

Jeanne patted her arm. 'I'd be grateful for that, Cora. I'm planning to tell Maggie in a few weeks' time.' She winked. 'To put your mind at rest, I've been secretly married to my lovely architect husband for over a twelve-month now and we're thrilled to bits about our coming event. I was worried about morning sickness but fortunately I got off lightly, apart from some queasiness. I had to tell the hostesses I flew with that I'd eaten too much rich food.'

'It must've been difficult for you.' Cora's thoughts whirled. How amazing to be keeping such a personal and precious secret.

Jeanne withdrew a thin gold chain from beneath her blue blouse. 'My wedding ring,' she said. 'Always with me, yet never on view. I'll have to resign of course, before people start noticing my expanding waistline. But I've enjoyed my years with Castle.' She glanced at the door. 'There's Shirley. She has an unaccompanied child with her and hasn't noticed us yet.'

'Don't worry. Mum's the word,' said Cora. 'Whoops, sorry!'

Jeanne chuckled. 'Thank you. I've enjoyed our time together. You'll go far, Cora. Mark my words.'

The office was filling with aircrew. Questions were asked. People made phone calls. Shirley, clutching her young charge's hand, looked tense on recognising Jeanne, though the Newcastle-based skipper greeted the check hostess warmly and proudly produced his daughter's first school photograph to show her.

'Were you nervous?' Shirley drew Cora aside. 'What sort of things does she expect?'

'It was fine,' said Cora. 'Just act as normal but don't offer her coffee until you've served everyone else.'

Jeanne approached them. 'I guess Cora has explained what I'm up to, Shirley.' She smiled at the unaccompanied child travelling in the airline's care and crouched beside her. 'Hello, sweetheart. That's a pretty doll. What's her name?'

'Rosebud,' said the little girl, her eyes solemn. 'Did you know she has to be strapped in with me before the captain can take off?'

'Goodness! No, I didn't,' said Jeanne. 'Maybe I could tell you and Rosebud a story later when Shirley's busy?'

★   ★   ★

The southbound crew checked in at a central Liverpool hotel. 'We'll have something to eat here,' said Bing

Crosby. 'Unless you young things fancy a nightclub. I hear the place to be is, um, the Pink Parrot?'

'Perish the thought,' said Tony. 'I hate those places but I'll make the effort for you, Cora.'

'You're off the hook,' she said. 'I guess it'll be an early start tomorrow.'

'You drew the short straw this week,' said the first officer.

'I'm pleased my check's over and done with. Learning stuff for the written exam's one thing, but juggling trays and keeping a smile on your face is the hard part.'

'Pull the other one,' said Bing. 'You're a natural, young lady. I told Jeanne you were nippy round the cabin. Now, the restaurant closes in half an hour, so shall we go straight in? They'll keep our bags at reception. First, I must wash my hands.'

As they walked towards the dining room, Tony turned to Cora. 'Last time I flew with Jeanne,' he said, 'I remember she couldn't eat anything when we went out to lunch. She looked very drawn and someone said she'd been off colour for a while.' He hesitated. 'There's a rumour going around and I'd hate to think of her being wrongly accused of something.'

'What kind of something?' Cora asked.

Tony coloured up. 'I don't need to spell it out, surely? These things happen but we're talking about someone the younger hostesses look up to.'

Cora gathered her thoughts swiftly. 'Jeanne told me she'd been poorly but I think that was down to a stomach bug.' She mentally crossed her fingers. 'She seems fine now.'

'Flying can take its toll,' said Tony, looking relieved.

'I'm beginning to discover that,' said Cora, thankfully sinking into a chair.

12

Next day, after aeroplanes and crews landed in the right places, Cora travelled back in Tony's car.

'In case you wondered,' he said, 'you, me and Bing are together for the foreseeable future.'

'That's a relief,' she said. 'Although I don't have anything against Captain Tracey.'

'What about his first officer?'

'You mean Ross?'

'Who else?'

'I'm not sure what I'm supposed to say.'

'Oh, come on. This is the elephant in the room, isn't it? You could cut the atmosphere between the two of you with a knife. It started at the Beehive and it's continuing. I do wish that friend of mine wouldn't play games. Maybe it's time I reminded him he has

a fiancée. Maybe it's time you remembered too.'

Cora felt helpless, unable to defend
Ross or herself. She stared straight
ahead, cheeks burning while traffic
slowed for the bridge to part and allow
a boat to sail beneath. She waited until
the car glided to a halt. 'You've no
business saying such a thing.'

'Probably not. But it needs saying.
Friends should look out for one
another. We are friends, aren't we?'

'Of course,' she said. 'And you
shouldn't try and pressure me into
talking about another friend.'

He turned towards her. 'I've known
Ross a few years now. You're a much
newer friend, but I'm fond of you,
Cora. I'd hate to see you get hurt.'

'You're reading too much into this. If
you'd only seen Ross's reaction when
my ex-boyfriend turned up last Sunday
night, you'd change your tune. Ross
couldn't get away fast enough.'

'You've lost me.'

'Maybe I've lost everyone. I value

your friendship, Tony. But I'm not a bone to be picked over or some kind of trophy to win. My mother's trying to run my life and my former boyfriend's only keen to get me back because for some obscure reason he sees me as more interesting and glamorous than before.'

Slowly the two halves of the bridge descended and linked, giving traffic the green light. 'I understand and I'm sorry if I upset you,' said Tony. 'But I can't help my feelings.'

'Nor I, mine. Can we forget about Ross, please? Tell me about this plan of yours. Can anyone join?'

'Do you like messing about in boats?' Tony grinned happily. 'I fancy buying a houseboat and there's one for sale down at Saltford. Sorry to mention Ross again, but I was hoping he might come in with me. The way things are, maybe I'd better keep my mouth shut about his fiancée.'

'Do you mean you want to live on the river?'

'Possibly. We'd have to see what the accommodation's like for two single chaps. Summer's coming so we could have days out on the water. Cruise back in time for a meal at the pub. Idyllic. Very relaxing.'

'Two people flying alternate days,' she said.

'Yes, it would work perfectly. The one left on the boat could invite someone along for company.' He changed gear. 'If this comes off, maybe you'd like to join me sometimes.'

'It sounds fun,' she said.

'To say the old tub needs a facelift is an understatement, but I promise I'm not looking for a skivvy!'

'Just as well,' said Cora. 'Of course I'll help, but don't we see enough of each other when we're working?' As the words left her mouth she realised how hurtful that throwaway remark must have sounded.

'Thanks for the vote of confidence,' said Tony.

She glanced sideways and to her

relief saw him smile.

'I've got my eye on a captaincy one day, just as Ross has. But we need masses more experience. We need to watch and learn. Jump through the hoops. A hobby away from flying sounds perfect to me.' Tony turned into Cora's road and parked near the Jelly residence.

'Do you want to come in for a cuppa?'

'Only if you're sure.'

'I'm allowed visitors, you know.'

'Even ones you see enough of when you're flying with them?'

'I'll ignore that. Come and see my home. It's only a bedsit, but it's comfortable.'

'So's my place. Comfortable, I mean. But I have this yen to live on a boat and if Ross isn't keen, I wondered if he'd like to take over my room at the flat. It'd save Bill finding a replacement. Somehow I'll scrape together enough cash to buy the houseboat, with or without Ross's help.'

'When you were a child, was your favourite book *Wind in the Willows*?' she asked.

'Nope, try *Biggles*.'

'Ah,' said Cora, reaching for the door handle. 'It had to be one or the other.'

* * *

Ross had spent the night at his mother and stepfather's thatched cottage in Surrey. His dark green MG sports car needed elastic sides to accommodate the stuff he'd stored with his folks while he lived out of a suitcase. After moving from hotel to friend's lumpy sofa and back to hotel again while filling gaps in the roster, at last he had his posting. He was off to Bristol with the bonus of having his friend Tony from air training college already there, plus the opportunity to fly alongside the intrepid Captain George Tracey.

So, what about Cora? The attraction sparking between them the first time they'd exploded into each other's path still existed. Last weekend proved that, especially when they'd kissed beneath the starlit sky. Having confided his quandary to her, he also needed to explain himself to his friend. He must swallow his pride and tell Tony what prompted him to pretend his engagement still existed. Ross hated being laughed at but must endure any flak coming his way.

Approaching the level crossing over the branch line, he slowed, winding down his window to listen to the rumble and chuff of a steam train heading for the south coast. He watched the locomotive thunder by, recalling his childhood five minute fancy to become a train driver. Whereas his ambition to fly lasted and lasted, and he'd never stopped being proud of following in his father's footsteps.

One thing bothered him. He'd opened his heart to Cora in Reims but she'd said nothing about having a steady boyfriend. That fellow who turned up to meet her had looked daggers at him. Ross couldn't blame him. Any man would be proud to have Cora as his girlfriend.

The long-standing ambition to take the controls of a transatlantic jet airliner still burned brightly. He'd already made one enormous mistake in the romance department, so why did he go on dreaming about Cora, with her quirky sense of humour and sparkling brown eyes? OK, he'd kissed her and she'd kissed him back. Maybe she was a flirt? How did the boyfriend view her career? How long would he be prepared to wait before clipping her wings and whisking her away to a thatched cottage with roses round the door? The thought filled Ross with gloom.

* * *

'Dave's no longer my boyfriend, Mum. I thought you realised.'

'I hope you know what you're doing, Cora. How do you even know the airline will keep you on after the summer season?' Arlene Murray banged her rolling pin on the marble pastry board.

'I don't for certain, but I very much hope they will. What's that got to do with whether or not I have a boyfriend?' Cora went on searching for the can of pie filling her mother needed.

'Try behind the baked beans on the top shelf,' said Arlene. 'Look, love. That young man thinks the world of you. I happened to bump into him down town and all he could talk about was you and whether I thought you'd allow him a second chance. I didn't see any harm in giving him some encouragement.'

'You shouldn't have tried guessing my working days, Mum. Thanks to you, Dave booked into a guest house for the night only to find I wouldn't be around next day.'

Thump, thump, went the rolling pin.

'And another thing,' said Cora. 'He's only taking such an interest because his last girlfriend decided she preferred someone else. He likes the thought of going out with a girl who wears an eye-catching blue uniform. In his misguided way, he sees me as a better catch than before I started flying. He thinks he's in love but I know better than that.'

'Do you indeed? Well, I think he's probably seen sense. My guess is he missed you while he was courting that other girl and now he's seen the error of his ways. Everyone makes mistakes.'

Cora reached for the tin opener. 'Maybe so, but I'm happy as I am. I've already made new friends. I'm going to the cinema again sometime with a girl who works at the airport, once she stops working the late shift and I'm not on the schedule.'

Arlene Murray sniffed. 'That's exactly what I mean. Your unpredictable hours mean you ignore your old friends. You don't have set meal times either — that can't be good for your constitution.'

Cora burst out laughing. 'Mum, you're priceless!' She hugged Arlene. 'I often worked long hours at Gigi's, including most Saturdays, as you very well know. As for old friends, well, they're thin on the ground nowadays.'

'Careful, or you'll get flour over your dress. Take an apron from the top drawer, then you can grate an apple in with the cherry filling. Your dad likes that.'

'I'll open the gate, shall I?'

'Yes, please. I'd almost forgotten.'

'It wouldn't be the end of the world if you did, Mum,' Cora said gently. Her mother thrived on routine and in her younger days, her home life and expectations had enormously differed from those of her daughter now.

'Are you staying the night, love?'

'If you'll have me,' said Cora. 'Otherwise I'll hardly see anything of Dad. I'm not flying tomorrow but I have a hair appointment in the afternoon.'

'I wonder if . . . '

Cora glanced at her mother. Arlene looked rather flustered. Maybe she'd been about to suggest ringing Dave.

Surely no one could be that blatant?

Outside, Cora glanced up and noticed a vapour trail painting a white stripe in the sky. It would be the evening scheduled flight on its way over the Bristol Channel. How strange to think of people she knew up there while she gazed at the rapidly vanishing wisp. Cora opened the gates wide and went indoors again. Thank goodness she was back quickly, putting paid to any chance of Arlene sending Dave a smoke signal. Oh, the joys of being an only child and a daughter whose mum's expectations for her didn't match her own!

This thought reminded her of Ross, who'd no doubt sympathise. Except he was a man, and men's mums didn't necessarily dream of white weddings like girls' mums did.

* * *

'It doesn't exactly live up to its name, does it?' Cora couldn't help giggling.

215

'Some people might say a boat called *High Flyer* was perfect for a pilot. Anyway, a rub-down and a lick of paint work wonders,' said Tony.

Cora looked down at her feet. 'A bit of baling out wouldn't come amiss. I'm standing in a half-inch of water here.'

'Good point. I'll see if the owner will knock something off the price.'

'I know nothing about boats, but I imagine you'd need to drag this one out of the water for a hull inspection?'

'One of the customs officers at the airport knows everything worth knowing. But what do you think of the idea in principle?'

They clambered back on deck. 'It's a lovely place,' said Cora. 'Trust you to find something close to the pub.'

'Handy for meals when I can't be bothered to cook,' said Tony.

'Well, I wish you luck if it's what you want.' She longed to ask whether he'd approached his friend but resisted the impulse.

'Ross says he's interested,' said Tony,

216

as if mind-reading. 'He's coming to look her over on Sunday after his flight.'

'If you go ahead with this, surely it'd be ages before you could move in?'

'You'd be surprised. But we won't do anything rash. Ross is kipping on our settee. It's far from ideal, given our working hours, but it'll do for now.'

They sat down on a low wall.

'To be honest, my flatmate isn't over the moon about it, even though he gets on well with Ross,' said Tony. 'Problem is, it's not so easy when Ross is ready to turn in and Bill's still watching the TV. If you hear of a room going for a short let, maybe you could let me know?'

Cora knew her landlord had been disappointed at the last minute by a prospective tenant, but how would her suggestion look? She didn't even know if Ross had confessed his broken engagement to Tony yet. It seemed mean not to speak out. 'There's a room free on the floor below mine,' she said. 'He'll need to be quick off the mark because I think the advert goes in the evening paper tomorrow.'

'I see.' Tony stared at the gently lapping water.

'Do you?'

'It seems too good to be true,' said Tony. 'I suppose you must like the idea, or you wouldn't have suggested it.'

'It makes no difference to me,' said Cora. 'I'm hardly likely to see much of him, the way our work patterns are.'

'True. You know, he's a fussy chap when it comes to his living quarters. Says he much prefers camping out at a friend's place to living in some grotty bedsit with dodgy neighbours.'

She nodded gravely. 'So you reckon he wouldn't be interested in Laurel Road?'

'Ha ha! Your place is tip-top. Even Ross couldn't quibble over it. But are you quite sure about this?'

'I doubt I'll even know he's around, and I certainly won't be leaving homemade cakes outside his door if that's what you're thinking.'

'He's told me about Nicole, you

know,' said Tony. 'He also said he'd let the cat out of the bag to you.'

'Well, now you know I can keep a secret.'

'Yep. You're a pal. I'd hate for Bill to get fed up and give Ross his marching orders.' Tony checked his watch. 'The crew should be back at the airport now. I can ask to speak to him or leave a message.'

'At least you haven't far to walk to the phone box.' Cora pointed to the pub.

'And here are all the airline office numbers.' Tony tapped his jeans pocket.

'I'm impressed.' She stood up. 'I think I can manage to remember the phone number of my house.'

He grabbed her hand and broke into a jog. 'If you can't remember it, I can.'

'I might've known. If your friend's interested, tell him to give Mr Jelly a ring around ten in the morning.'

'Are you kidding me? He's to ring a Mr Jelly?'

'That's right.' She pulled her hand

free. 'And tell Ross not to make silly jokes. My landlord's already heard them all.'

'Yes, ma'am,' said Tony.

★ ★ ★

A couple of days later, Cora went downstairs to find Mr Jelly on the doorstep, polishing the brass knocker.

'I'm glad I saw you,' he said. 'First Officer Anderson took one look at the room and agreed to rent it on a month-by-month basis. Thanks very much, Miss Murray. He seems a pleasant young man.'

Cora swallowed. 'I'm pleased to have helped. How's your wife's knee now?'

'Much improved. I've told her not to climb even the smallest step ladder in future.' He sighed. 'She can be very impatient sometimes.'

'I expect she likes things just so.' Cora shuddered. 'I twisted my knee years ago playing hockey. So I know all about the pain of a cartilage injury.'

'It's not nice for poor Cherry. I'll tell her you asked. Don't forget to pick up your mail.'

Cora didn't know where to look. She nodded, desperately trying to stop her lips twitching as she picked up her letters. Walking away from the house, she smiled at the thought of a lady called Cherry marrying a Mr Jelly. It certainly must liven up the doctor's waiting room when Mrs J's name was called.

Her mum had redirected one letter. The other bore her name but was addressed in unfamiliar writing. Cora ripped open the first one and found a birth announcement. Her former manager, Em, was proud mum to baby Melissa, weighing in at 6lbs 4 ounces. Cora made a mental note to add a congratulations card to her shopping list. She'd a shrewd idea about the other envelope, a brown one, which the sender had probably acquired from the Castle Airways office.

Ross had written a brief memo

thanking her for alerting him about the bedsit. He said he hoped to see her soon and sent his best wishes. Cora heaved a sigh. With any luck, that meeting wouldn't happen yet awhile. She stuffed both envelopes into her handbag and set off in search of something tasty for supper.

But she had to pass one of her favourite stores. And in its window she saw the most delectable dress, so beautiful that it beckoned her to try it on. Cora smiled, noticing the mannequin's wig, identical to her own hairstyle.

She wandered inside, asked to see the red dress in the window and enjoyed the feeling of not having to concern herself with end-of-season sales and shifting stock. She was turning away from the counter when she noticed a figure wearing the familiar Castle Airways blue.

'Shirley!' Cora hurried forward.

'Gosh, how lovely to see you. I've been meaning to ask if you wanted to meet up some time.'

'What have you done with your crew?'

'Tony Cullen's taken them to see a houseboat he's interested in. He collected us from the airport. I was glad of the lift but I thought I'd leave the boys to their fun.'

'Very wise,' said Cora. 'Do you fancy a coffee? There's a restaurant here.'

'Let's take the escalator,' said Shirley. 'You can show me what you've bought.'

Over a pot of coffee and plate of buttered toast, the two compared notes.

'You know I flew out of Gatwick last weekend?'

'I heard,' said Cora. 'Someone went sick?'

'That's right. For some reason, Jeanne Whitfield's doing office duties and the standby hostess sprained her ankle, so I got the call to hop on the London train.'

'Who was your number one?'

223

'Would you believe, Maggie Martin?'

'And you survived?' Cora picked up a slice of toast. 'Oh dear, she wouldn't approve of this.'

'But we need to think of our energy levels! Yes, I was nervous at first, but Maggie was great. I loved it. Can't wait to do another!'

Cora wondered how much longer Jeanne could keep her secret. 'So you'll be hoping for a Gatwick posting one day?'

'Perhaps,' said Shirley. 'Between you and me, I'm planning to apply to a bigger airline at the end of the year.'

'Good for you,' said Cora. 'If that's what you want.'

'How about you?'

'Me? Oh, I'd love an occasional trip out of Gatwick. But I like being based in Bristol, especially as I've got a great little bedsit. If Castle decide to keep me, I'll do the winter schedule and study Spanish or Italian at night school.'

'Why wouldn't they keep you?'

'Well, they can't keep everybody on for the autumn and winter, can they? Anyway, we're only just starting the busy season.'

'It's good to have your sights set on something.'

Cora thought of Ross and his ambitions. 'I suppose so.' People often told her their secrets. Maybe she invited confidences. Unlike Shirley, she really didn't want to think too hard about the future when she was enjoying the now.

They gossiped about one or two of their intake, girls clearly hoping to find a pilot husband. Shirley giggled. 'Just for fun, which one would you marry, if you had to?'

'Captain Crosby,' said Cora. 'He's such a kind man. Happily wed, so don't get any ideas.'

Shirley raised her eyebrows. 'Are you sure there's no one among the first officers?'

But Cora wouldn't rise to the bait. 'Ask me when I'm 29,' she joked.

Riding the down escalator after their snack, Cora watched shoppers' heads turn, noticing Shirley in her uniform. 'People probably wonder what a glam girl like you is doing with a nobody like me,' she said.

'If they only knew! I heard on the grapevine, both Bristol-based first officers are vying for your attentions.'

'Now that really is silly gossip.'

'Tony Cullen's not the one that's engaged, is he?'

'No. Ross Anderson was, but not anymore.'

'Ah,' said Shirley knowingly.

Cora stepped off the escalator behind her. 'I see a lot of Tony because we're crewed together. He's like a big brother.'

'I believe you, but thousands wouldn't!' Shirley consulted her watch. 'I'll finish looking around, then head for the bus stop.'

'OK. It's been good to see you.'

'We must do it again, pet. Maybe one day you'd like to come and sit in my garden in Ponteland? After things warm up, of course.'

'Sorry?'

Shirley chuckled. 'I meant the weather, pet. What did you think I meant?'

13

Cora wasn't expecting events to catapult her from her usual routine. One Monday morning she was roused by the sound of loud knocking on her door.

'Miss Murray, wake up! You're needed at the airport.'

Still foggy with sleep, Cora pushed back the bedclothes and pattered to the door. She unfastened the safety chain and stuck out a tousled head.

Cherry Jelly stood there, hair covered by an orange chiffon turban and wearing a sunburst kimono. 'You're being called into work. The other girl isn't well enough to fly. They say to take a taxi to the airport.'

'What time is it?'

'Half past six. What time shall I tell the taxi firm?'

'You are kind, Mrs Jelly. Seven o'clock sharp, please.'

On arrival, Cora hurtled into the office, totally ignoring rules regarding hostesses hurrying. She stopped short at the sight of her pale-faced, woebegone friend.

'I'm so sorry,' said Wendy. 'I daren't fly, not with this horrible cold.'

'You sound terrible! You're off the hook but I'll need to get a move on.'

'I've already checked Pappa and everything's in order. All you have to do is walk on board.'

'Thanks for being so thoughtful,' said Cora. 'Go home to bed now, you poor thing.'

She headed outside to where the Dakota sat in the morning sunshine. She'd been busy during the cab ride, pinning up her hair, hiding most of it beneath her cap. She hadn't had time for a shampoo. She hadn't even had time to think, given the driver's curiosity about her job.

So when Ross Anderson loped up the steps and entered the cabin, she looked

229

at him as if she'd never seen him before in her life.

'Wendy's not well enough to fly, I gather?'

'She's very poorly,' said Cora, avoiding his eyes. Meeting that blue-eyed gaze was never easy, especially on a morning when she should still be snuggled under her eiderdown.

He picked up her vanity case. 'Let me stow this for you.'

She watched him swing the case up to the luggage rack. He turned towards her, catching her frozen in the moment, her eyes not meeting his, but gazing at his lips. Her heartbeat raced, her mouth dried, and her only thought was dismay. How professional and sophisticated was this?

'Your hair's different,' he said softly.

'Desperation,' she said. 'I got ready in a rush.'

'You'd never know.'

'Um, I'd better check the cabin.'

'I think Wendy's already done it,' he said.

'Ah.'

'I didn't imagine we'd be crewed together so soon.'

'No,' she said, meeting his eyes at last.

'Cora, I . . . I'll see you later.' He began walking towards the cockpit.

'Stupid, stupid, stupid,' she muttered, tipping chunks of wrapped barley sugar on to a tiffin tray. 'How are you going to cope now, Miss Clever Sticks? Not only have you encouraged this man to move into the same house as you, but fate has also manoeuvred you into the same aeroplane.'

She told herself not to be such a drip. She needed to put all thoughts of First Officer Anderson out of her mind, Robert Redford look-alike or not.

The strains of 'Oh What a Beautiful Morning' floated up the steps. Captain Tracey stopped at sight of Cora.

'Air Hostess Murray,' he said. 'How fortunate I am to have two such delightful young ladies available as my crew.'

Cora, still a little in awe of the senior pilot, shook her head at him. 'Well, this young lady is trying to recover from an early morning wake-up call on her day off. It's good to see you again though, Captain.'

He headed towards the cockpit, calling over his shoulder, 'Don't forget I like custard creams, Cora. That's the way to a man's heart — remembering what his favourite biscuits are.'

* * *

Cora placed a tray on the console between the pilots. Beyond the windshield, endless cornflower-blue sky stretched as the Dakota gently climbed.

'You're quick off the mark,' said George Tracey.

Ross glanced down. 'Pink wafers? Do I look like a pink wafer kind of chap?'

'Eat what you're given, young fellow,' said George, turning to wink at Cora.

'No one can expect to have Bourbon biscuits or custard creams every time,' said Cora in her best Joyce Grenfell voice.

'No, miss. Sorry, miss,' said Ross meekly.

Cora swallowed a bubble of mirth. 'Wendy may spoil you,' she said sternly, 'but I've no intention of doing so.'

'I notice the captain gets his favourites,' said Ross gloomily.

Cora returned to the cabin. There was a mere sprinkling of passengers, but the aircraft would leave Liverpool with a full load. She'd time for a brief chat with two or three of the regulars, even topping up a coffee cup here and there — impossible when every seat was taken.

She'd have been horrified to hear the cockpit conversation after she left.

'Lovely lass,' said George Tracey. 'What was all that with the biscuits?'

'Um, I'm really not sure,' said Ross. He bit into a pink wafer.

'I doubt that. Come on, give me a little excitement in my life.'

'Let's say Cora and I got off on the

wrong foot. But she's just done me a good turn. She alerted me about a room to rent in the house she lives in.'

'Great Scott, man! That doesn't sound to me like getting off on the wrong foot.' The captain peered to the right. 'You sure about your flight plan? I don't recognise the starboard landscape.'

Ross grinned, aware how the skipper liked to challenge his first officers. He reeled off a navigational sequence.

'Just keeping my eye on the ball,' said George. 'So, your acquaintanceship with the lovely Miss Murray is progressing, soon to be enhanced?'

'Hardly,' said Ross. He cleared his throat. 'I suppose you know all about my former engagement?'

'I do. I've already heard the story from several people.'

'The upshot of it is, people were commenting about me becoming too friendly with a hostess while I was engaged to be married. I confessed to Cora how I'd avoided telling the truth about my fiancée and me splitting up and she and me, I mean Cora and I, were getting on swimmingly, but then she seemed to back off. Crikey, I'm making a pig's ear of this, Skipper.'

'You are, but it's not surprising. We're better at handling aeroplanes than women, but they're nowhere near as warm and cuddly.'

'It's certainly difficult, knowing how to deal with this situation. I've asked her to come out with me but I doubt she will.'

'I should try and dissuade you from taking things further, I suppose. In-house romance and all that,' said the captain. 'The truth is, pilots sometimes fall for air hostesses and vice versa.'

'Cora knows I'm working towards promotion and I think she's afraid of distracting me. But she already has.' He gulped his coffee.

'There's a time and a place for everything. Just bear that in mind. Everything will add up if it's meant to. I take it you're not thinking of proposing marriage just yet?'

'Crikey, no. Cora's taken to flying like that thing that goes quack-quack takes to water, and she's not going to give up her job in a hurry. Besides, there seems to be a boyfriend hanging around.'

'A woman like that's worth waiting for, young fellow. Make your feelings known if you don't want to lose her. Maybe it's exactly what she's hoping you'll do.'

★ ★ ★

Newcastle wore a cloak of drizzle by the time the crew reached the city, having accepted a lift from a fireman coming off duty. Captain Tracey was meeting one of his many friends from way back, leaving Cora and Ross outside the railway station. She didn't know whether she wanted the first officer to mumble an excuse and melt into the crowds or whether she wanted him to suggest they lunched together.

'Am I forgiven?'

'Forgiven for what?'

'For not being entirely honest, right from the start.'

'About your engagement? It really is none of my business, Ross. You did what you thought best.'

'Only after I realised how much I was attracted to you.'

Cora clenched her fists at her sides. 'I'm actually very hungry and I need some lunch,' she said. 'Breakfast wasn't on the agenda this morning.'

'I'm sorry. Let me make amends. There's a place nearby where they make fantastic omelettes.'

'With chips? I seriously fancy chips.'

He laughed and gently steered her by the elbow. 'I don't know how you stay so slim. Does Maggie Martin issue host-esses with magic pills by any chance?'

Cora, though loving his old-fashioned courtesy, didn't melt too quickly. 'We don't scoff biscuits like you pilots do,' she said primly.

'Did you know the pink ones taste

better than they look?' He didn't wait for an answer. 'Cora . . . '

'Yes?'

'Oh, nothing. Let's cross over. You shall have your omelette with chips and we'll talk about everything under the sun except ourselves. Will that suit you?'

'Very well, thank you.'

* * *

Cora flew her normal schedule next day, relieved to be off to Rotterdam with 'her boys', as she'd taken to calling Tony and Bing. When they returned to base that night, the station manager reported Wendy's doctor had signed her off from flying duties for two weeks.

'Poor girl,' said Cora. 'They daren't risk her eardrums being damaged. What's happening about the roster?'

'You have to do every single scheduled flight.' Tony kept a straight face.

Cora poked him in the ribs. 'I think not. We may not have a union like you

238

pilots, but Maggie's too considerate to let that happen.'

'There's a hostess coming from Gatwick,' mumbled the station manager through a mouthful of Mars bar. 'She's on the freighter due in this evening.'

'Really? We heard on the radio it was about twenty minutes behind us.' Tony looked at Cora. 'Do you want to wait?'

'It could be anyone,' she said. 'Someone I don't know. But it'd be a friendly thing to do. She'll be allowed a taxi to her hotel, though, Tony. You don't have to hang around.'

The first officer hesitated. 'I can take you both if one of you doesn't mind squeezing into the back.'

'You can get a whole crew in a mini,' said Cora.

'We've already booked a cab,' said the station manager, hiding a yawn. 'The freighter pilots are night-stopping.'

'Well, there we are,' said Tony. 'Problem solved, and any excuse for a party.'

Helen greeted Cora warmly and insisted on sitting in the back of Tony's car.

'Your protégé's doing fine, Helen. She keeps us all well in order,' Tony called over his shoulder. 'First Officer Anderson calls her the Biscuit Monitress.'

'Really?'

'I'm not nearly so strict as I should be,' said Cora.

'You'd better clue me in on this,' said Helen. 'I can continue whatever this joke is, tomorrow.'

Cora chuckled. 'That'd be fun. So many pilots like Bourbon creams, I told Ross Anderson yesterday that he wasn't allowed any.'

'And there we are on the flight deck, battling the elements, and you begrudge a brave aviator a few crumbs of biscuit,' said Tony.

'Well, don't go letting on to Ross that we're in league over the crew rations,' said Helen.

Tony muttered beneath his breath. 'Oh, all right then. What hope do I have against two such powerful women?'

'I bet you didn't think you'd be back so soon?' Cora glanced back at Helen.

'No, it'll seem strange, staying in a hotel instead of my old flat.'

'Make the most of it,' said Tony.

'Which captain am I crewed with tomorrow?' Helen asked.

'George Tracey,' said Tony.

'I haven't flown with him for quite a while.' Helen paused. 'I hope I'll see something of you two while I'm around.'

Cora held her breath. It was like being catapulted into a soap opera. She knew whose company Helen really craved, but how would Tony cope with this suggestion?

'We'll have to see,' said Tony. 'You know how it is.'

'Yes. I know,' said Helen. 'Well, sometimes fate works in strange ways.'

Cora made her decision. 'Tony, could you drop me off at the end of Laurel

Road, please? I don't want to be a spoilsport but I could sleep for a week.'

'Are you sure?'

'As long as you and Helen don't think I'm being unsociable.'

'Not at all,' said Helen. 'I don't want a late night either — just something light to eat and a glass of milk will do.'

'Such a glamorous lifestyle it is we lead,' said Tony.

*   *   *

When Cora and Tony flew together next, she'd caught up with her sleep. 'I didn't wake until eleven yesterday morning,' she said.

'Good job I didn't call for you on my way to the boat, then.'

'I hope you didn't think I was rude, not going to the hotel with you.'

'No. Amazingly, Helen and I cleared the air over certain matters.' He glanced at the door. 'Let's talk later. There's something you should know.'

Cora could hardly contain her

impatience but Tony hurried away to carry out his duties. After lunch at the airport, Bing decided he'd take a nap in the crew room, leaving Tony and Cora the opportunity to wander outside for a stroll.

'The fact is, Cora,' said Tony, 'there's gossip going around.'

'Isn't there always?'

'Of course. Jeanne Whitfield and whether or not she has a problem continues to intrigue some people.'

'People should mind their own business,' said Cora. 'Jeanne's like most of us. She has values. I'm sure she wouldn't step out of line.'

Tony cleared his throat. 'I'm sorry to sound cynical, but they say there's no smoke without fire. Unfortunately you, me and Ross seem to be another topic of speculation.'

Oh, for Jeanne's news to break! People really would have something to talk about then. Cora stopped walking. 'What exactly are people saying?'

'Helen asked me outright whether

you and me were seeing each other outside of work.'

'I'm sorry if I landed you with an awkward situation, but I could tell she wanted to be alone with you,' said Cora. 'And I wasn't fibbing when I said I really did need to sleep.'

'Everything was fine. She's changed a lot and we're much more relaxed together now. Helen knows you and I are good friends who sometimes meet on our days off.'

'And?' Cora glanced sideways at him. He sounded more relaxed too. 'Shall we walk on?'

'In a minute. Please don't be angry, but somehow people have the impression that Ross and I are rivals where you're concerned. That's the best way I can put it.'

'Is that how Helen put it?'

'That's exactly how she put it.'

'Which means,' she said, 'that other people are more outspoken. I heard something similar from Shirley.'

'Maybe I should tackle Ross and find

out once and for all whether he also thinks you and I are more than good friends?'

'Let's go back now, shall we? Let's hope this gossip fizzles out, because there's nothing between Ross and me. Get it? Neither of us is interested in any sort of relationship except a friendly working one. Exactly like you and me.'

She stalked ahead, fortunately unaware of the quizzical smile on Tony's face as he stared after her.

* * *

Cora waited for a totally free day before visiting her folks. On the way back to the station, she called on her former boss.

'Oh, Cora.' Em drew the soft red velvet dress from its tissue paper. 'This is beautiful.'

'Not as beautiful as your baby,' Cora said, cradling little Melissa. 'I deliberately went for a bigger size so hopefully it'll fit her by the winter. I don't expect you miss work at all, do you?'

'Not one bit,' said Em. 'I suppose one day I might, but certainly not at the moment. This little one keeps me pretty busy. But tell me all about you. No regrets?'

'None at all. My ex-boyfriend would've been a problem if I'd stayed at home.'

'Surely he wasn't harassing you?'

'It's more likely to be my mum harassing me on his behalf. I know lots of girls would give up chocolate for a steady fellow like Dave, but he and I aren't right for one another, whether or not I wear a gold wing on my jacket.'

'Of course it's easier for you to keep your distance now you're living away from home,' said Em, scooping up the lacy bundle and placing Melissa gently in her cot.

'I can do without complications. I have enough already.'

'You can talk to me if you want,' said Em. 'Not that I know anything about aviation.'

'It's not about aviation, it's about men — or one man in particular.'

'A pilot?'

'A first officer with blue, blue eyes, and he keeps distracting me.'

'That sounds like a delicious distraction to me,' said Em. 'Unless he's unavailable.'

'Hah! We're both unavailable. He has his sights set on a captaincy and I've only been flying a few months and don't intend letting anything throw me off track.'

'And what does this blue-eyed boy make of your decision?'

Cora reached for a biscuit. 'I can't resist homemade shortbread.'

'It's mum's special recipe. Don't change the subject.'

'OK. We met on my very first day . . . '

Em listened closely as Cora talked, sometimes nodding, sometimes raising her eyebrows and finally sitting back and sighing.

'The thought of that first kiss in a

beautiful French cathedral city — your life certainly has changed.'

'But don't you see that's just froth, Em? Whatever sparked between Ross and me happened when we bumped into each other on my very first day of training. I really wasn't looking for romance! Oh, I wish I could take a falling out of love pill, I really do.' Cora glanced guiltily at the cradle.

'Don't worry. Melissa won't wake up. But I think you should.'

'What do you mean?'

'Wake up, is what I mean. Forgive me for being blunt, but I think you're not being very adult about this. You're allowing this distraction, as you call him, to affect your life which otherwise, I think you'd agree, is pretty darned good.'

'Yes,' admitted Cora.

'You mentioned Ross asking if you'd like to go for a meal some time when you were both off duty.'

'Not a good idea.'

'I think it's an excellent idea,' said

Em. 'You're both behaving like teenagers. You need to talk things through. Go on a date or two. Spend time helping clean up this houseboat you mentioned. See how you enjoy each other's company away from the spotlight.'

'That hadn't occurred to me,' said Cora slowly. 'We're always on show at work. People look at us because we're in uniform. Other crew members notice if we spend time together.' *Especially if they catch us sharing a kiss!* 'I'm much easier in Tony Cullen's company — in any of the other pilot's company!'

'Another thing,' said Em. 'How long did you say you'd known Ross before he mentioned his fake engagement?'

'Minutes.'

'And when you first met, something clicked between you? Something apart from bumping into one another?'

'Yes. Something tummy-lurching and tingly.'

'Oh dear,' said Em. 'You definitely have a problem, don't you?'

14

Cora's next flight was a charter to Amsterdam. A choir was travelling to Holland for a tour and they exercised their vocal chords during takeoff, something which passengers seated towards the front probably didn't hear above the engine noise. Cora enjoyed listening to 'Tulips from Amsterdam' but was kept busy serving drinks, tasty open sandwiches and the sort of sticky, delicious Danish pastries certain pilots would kill for.

The turn-around time was brief, giving Cora no opportunity for sightseeing. 'Have you ever explored the city?' she asked Ross as they walked across the tarmac.

'I have. There's plenty of history. Amsterdam, like so many other cities, is a mix of medieval buildings and modern ones. You'd like the shops.'

'I expect so. I wish we were night-stopping.'

'Me too.'

She kept abreast of him, her tone deliberately light. 'We must have that meal together soon.'

'Must we?' He sounded frighteningly aloof.

'I thought you wanted — I mean, I thought you might be waiting for me to suggest it,' she said without conviction.

'You mustn't feel obligated, Cora.'

'I don't. I wish I hadn't said anything now.' She bit her lip, feeling snubbed.

'I'm trying not to make a nuisance of myself,' he said quietly.

They stopped, allowing a tractor pulling a baggage trolley to cross their path.

'You're not a nuisance,' she said.

'Oh, I think I am,' said Ross. 'I keep popping up in your life.'

'We work for the same airline!'

'Believe me, I go for months without seeing certain colleagues. But with you and me at the same base, we can hardly avoid being crewed together some- times.'

'What are you saying? Should I request a transfer?'

'Of course not! Can't you realise, that's the last thing I want?' The emotion in his voice almost made Cora well up. Yet, moments before, he'd seemed so distant. She stood still, airport life going on all around them, until he spoke again.

'We'd better get out of the line of fire.'

If only it was that easy, thought Cora, following him inside the airport build- ing. Ross had only just gained his hoped-for posting. She was finding her feet in a job she loved more and more every single time she climbed the steps into her beloved aeroplane. Yet how was either of them to find peace of mind if they persisted in burying their feelings for one another?

★ ★ ★

Cora boarded the Dakota as soon as the porters finished stowing the passenger luggage beside the galley. She made her way to the front of the aircraft, where the flight engineer greeted her through the open door.

'You're in luck, Jock,' she said. 'Plenty of food left.'

'Music to my ears,' he said.

'Why are flight crews always ravenous?'

He shrugged. 'Boredom?'

Cora chuckled. 'Better a boring flight than the other sort,' she said.

'You're learning fast,' said Jock.

She bent down and picked up something from the floor, balancing it in the palm of one hand. 'The initials R.A.,' she said. 'I'll hand it to him, shall I?'

Jock pointed behind her. 'Himself is on his way now.'

Cora turned and held out the slim silver pen to the first officer. Ross's stern expression at once lightened.

'Wow,' he said. 'I've only just realised

it was missing. Thanks, Cora. It means a lot to me.'

'A gift?'

'It belonged to my father. It hasn't worked for ages but I like to carry it on me.'

'You have the same initials,' she said.

'Yep. His name was Robert, known as Robbie.' He smiled at her. 'Thanks again. I'd better get on.'

'I'm sorry.' She moved aside.

'Please don't apologise,' he said.

'Isn't this where we came in?'

She met his gaze. They both chuckled and he didn't look away until she set off down the gangway, checking for anything out of place, but her mind still on Ross and how relieved he was to be handed his pen. Maybe he'd feared someone had pocketed it or that it had fallen somewhere inaccessible.

Flight CA702 left on time with 14 passengers, all sailors joining a ship at Liverpool. A tail wind helped whisk the Dakota along while Cora served drinks and snacks to crew and passengers, but a light load gave her time to sit for a while, watching the blanket of whipped-cream clouds below.

Atishoo! That sneezing sound had come from behind. But how could that be? Cora was sitting in a rear seat, with galley and small baggage hold behind her. She got up to investigate. The toilet was unoccupied and anyone wishing to use it must pass her anyway. Could an animal have wandered on board and be trapped somewhere? If so, why no mews or barks of distress?

She peered through the canvas webbing securing the luggage. One suitcase bulged awkwardly against the side. She looked more closely. Something wasn't quite right. Maybe she should call Jock to investigate. Uncertain whether she was being wise, she gingerly prodded the offending baggage.

Cora gasped as the webbing wobbled and her gaze met a pair of large, dark eyes. Startled eyes set in a small, pale face. 'How on earth did you get in there? And do you speak English?'

'It wasn't difficult,' he said. 'I wanted to see Grandma.'

'I see,' said Cora. 'Where does Grandma live?'

'Liverpool.'

'You knew which aeroplane to get on then, didn't you?'

'I've flown before with this airline, with my mum and dad.'

'Hmm. We'd better get you out of there and into a seat.' Cora inspected the webbing, noting how easy it must have been for the child to wriggle inside.

He looked mutinous. 'Can't I stay here?'

'I'm afraid not, love. I have to tell the captain there's an extra person on board and he'll want to know you're safe.'

'Must you tell him?'

'Don't be frightened. He can't make you get out!'

His eyes widened. 'Thank goodness! It's a long way to swim.'

Cora pulled at the webbing so her new passenger could climb through. She guided him to a seat, thoughts awhirl, imagining the boy's parents wondering where on earth their son had gone.

'What's your name, young man?' She kept her tone friendly.

'Brian Hansen.'

'And how old are you, Brian?'

'I'm ten.'

'Where do you live?'

'Not far from the airport.'

'So you walked there from your home?'

'Yes. I hung around 'til I heard a porter talk about the Liverpool flight. He said they were about to load the baggage so I followed him and hid behind another plane until the coast was clear.'

'You speak Dutch?'

'Yes. My dad's Dutch. Mum's English.'

'I bet you like adventure stories,' said Cora. 'And I bet you're hungry.'

'I brought some bread and cheese with me but I've eaten it already.'

'I'll fetch you an orange juice, then I must talk to the captain,' said Cora. 'When I come back, I'll find you something to eat and you can tell me your address and your grandma's address. Is that all right?'

'Super duper,' he said.

In the cockpit, Cora crouched beside Captain Tracey. 'You'll never guess what I've found,' she said, pitching her voice above the thrum of the engines.

'A diamond ring down the back of a seat?'

'Something much more precious. A little stowaway.'

George twisted round to face her. 'You're having me on!'

'No. Brian's ten and he's half English, half Dutch and lives not far from Amsterdam Airport. He has a grandma in Liverpool and decided to visit her.'

Ross burst out laughing. 'Cheeky little fellow. How the heck did he get away with it, I wonder?'

Cora explained. 'I'm going to give Brian something to eat now,' she said. 'I'll find out his home address so you can radio it. If someone alerts the local police, I imagine they'll inform his parents?'

'Affirmative,' said George. 'Ross, would you do the necessary as soon as Cora gets back to us?'

'Will do.'

'I'll bring more coffee and sandwiches soon,' she said.

Ross turned to face her. 'Cora, if you're running low on food, please give my share to the little chap.'

'Two's up on that,' said the captain. 'It probably hasn't occurred to Brian that he was breaking the law.'

'Anyway, how could anyone be cross with a little boy longing to see his grandma?' Ross chimed in.

Cora cleared her throat. 'Fortunately there's plenty of food left,' she said. 'But thank you. He's a delightful little boy.'

She found Brian gazing through the window. 'Everything's going to be fine,' she said. 'But we must let your mum and dad know your whereabouts.'

He bit his lip and nodded. 'I can give you our phone number.'

Cora reached for her notepad. 'Super,' she said. 'Something to eat now?'

'Please. I've got some guilders on me.'

Cora swallowed. He looked so vulnerable, sitting there in his check shirt and grey shorts. He'd taken off his dark blue windcheater. She couldn't imagine what the child's mum and dad must be going through but knew they'd hear good news very soon now.

'Don't worry about money, Brian.'

When she arrived in the cockpit again, Ross took the details from her.

'Bring the lad up front when it's convenient,' said George. 'I don't want to go back and draw attention to him. He can sit in the jump seat for a while.'

When Cora returned with the little

boy, Jock the engineer took charge of him. On her way down the cabin she accepted orders from passengers and busied herself in the galley, and was wondering whether to go back and collect the child when she noticed Ross making his way towards her.

'Do you want me to fetch Brian?' she asked him.

'In about ten minutes,' said Ross. 'He's sitting in my seat, wearing the headset and listening in to all the boring stuff.'

'You know very well it won't be boring to him.'

'At his age, I'd have given a year's sweet ration for such a chance.' His grin was wistful. 'He's a great kid. Very bright and obviously loves aeroplanes.'

'What about his parents?'

'They'd already contacted the police. By now, Brian's folks will know we have him and I imagine Grandma will be at Liverpool Airport, waiting to collect him.'

'What an adventure.' She shivered.

'But it gave me a turn, seeing a pair of eyes gazing back at me through the webbing.'

Ross caught his breath. 'Are you OK?'

She nodded.

'Good,' he said. 'I'd hate to think of you being upset in any way.' He reached out and tenderly touched her cheek.

Cora held her breath but the moment passed, leaving her gazing at the tall figure striding back down the cabin, stopping here and there to greet a passenger or answer a question. A little voice inside her seemed to put words into her mouth. A little voice saying, *don't ever let me go.* A little voice bringing thoughts of what Ross's son might look like.

* * *

Even though they lived under the same roof, Cora soon found how easy it was to ensure she didn't cross the path of someone who set her pulse racing in a very unladylike way. This someone was never far from her thoughts but she steeled herself not to allow the gorgeous young pilot to divert her from doing the job she loved.

She normally turned in around nine thirty the night before a duty day and imagined Ross never returned until much later. Thanks to her room being at the back of the house, away from the racket of banging doors and revving engines, she never heard a thing.

With long summer days now, Cora enjoyed time spent on the houseboat. To her delight, Tony often mentioned Helen, although she'd long returned to Gatwick and Wendy was working as hard as any of them, her illness well in the past. Sometimes she and Cora left notes in one another's pigeonholes at the Castle office, but with flights leaving Bristol seven days a week, the girls hardly ever met. Nor did Cora and Ross, but still she didn't attempt to make contact.

'You men are a funny lot,' said Cora

one day, unwrapping the picnic she'd brought to the houseboat.

'I've no idea what you mean by that remark, young lady,' said Tony as he placed two pints of cold lemonade on the cabin table.

'You don't seem so keen to move in here now.'

'Nope,' he said. 'I'm thinking of advertising the boat for hire once it's properly finished. Seems a shame to move out of Bill's flat. Ross seems happy where he is too. Not that we see much of each other these days.'

Cora didn't rise to that one. 'And another thing,' she said, waving a celery stick. 'You were like an awkward teenager around Helen when I first saw you two together. It was as if you were frightened of her.'

He rolled his eyes, bit into his ham roll and mumbled.

'Say that again, please!'

He swallowed. 'Sorry. I said, you were right. I didn't want to be tied down.'

'Exactly how I feel,' said Cora. 'But nowadays, Helen's name comes into the conversation quite a lot.'

'We do, um, speak a bit on the telephone. She's enjoying being based at Gatwick. I have to go across for a medical next week so I might, um, might actually see her then.'

'She's not flying that day?'

'She definitely has the day off.' He peered at Cora. 'Why are you looking at me like that?'

'I'm pleased for you, that's all.' She sipped her lemonade.

'I'm lucky she didn't go off me for good, the way I treated her. We're enjoying each other's company and taking things very, very slowly.' He eyed the picnic box. 'You're not eating much.'

'It's the warm weather. I'm not complaining though.'

'You've lost weight, haven't you? It must be love.'

'Here we go,' said Cora. 'Have another ham roll.'

'Cheers. So, how's the boyfriend these days?'

'For goodness sake, Dave isn't my boyfriend!'

Tony shot her an amused glance. 'It's odd how Ross still seems to think he is.'

Cora frowned. 'Have you two been discussing me?'

'Of course. You know, you girls really are a funny lot! Why do you let Ross go on thinking you're still seeing your ex?'

'It's ages since Dave turned up to collect me that time. I was cross with him for assuming what he had no business to assume.'

'You said Ross had already offered to drive you home.'

'But it would've been rude to snub Dave. He can't help being a pain, I suppose.'

'Instead, you snubbed Ross.' Tony glared at her.

She glared back. 'I did no such thing. He couldn't wait to find someone else to keep him company in his MG.'

266

'He told me you were the first person he'd confided in about that stupid pretence of his. He was honest with you.'

'Eventually,' said Cora.

'Now you seem to be using the same darned silly tactics over what's-his-name as Ross did over Nicole. Don't you think it's your turn to be honest?'

She thought of what Em had said. She thought back to the night when Dave turned up. She hadn't handled the situation well but to be fair, Ross had probably been embarrassed and, not knowing Cora's recent history, decided to back off. Her cheeks burned. How dreadful if he thought she juggled boyfriends like hairdressing appointments. Dave still wrote or rang now and then. Maybe she should heed the advice she'd been given.

'You've caught the sun,' Tony said gently. 'It suits you. Don't torture yourself, Cora. At least meet the fellow and clear up any misunderstandings. I hate to see my friends unhappy.'

'I'm not unhappy,' she protested.

'But you're not totally happy.'

'Are you asking me to answer that?'

'It's a fact, not a question,' said Tony.

15

Later that day, Cora wrote to Dave, thanking him for caring about her but telling him she regretted she couldn't reciprocate his feelings and had decided it best to make a clean break. Afterwards, she rang her mother to explain what she'd done.

'You don't seem surprised,' said Cora afterward.

'Your dad's been talking to me,' said Arlene. 'I'm sorry I reacted the way I did after you joined the airline, but I genuinely thought Dave was worth hanging on to, love.'

'I'm sure he is, Mum. But only by someone who truly cares for him. He'll find another girl. I think he was clinging to the past.'

'How are you getting on? Breaking hearts among the pilots?'

'No! I have one very good platonic

friend who I'm crewed with mostly. Otherwise I live a quiet life.'

'It seems odd hearing you say that,' said Arlene. 'You being an air hostess and flying here, there and everywhere.'

'It's not in the least glamorous, Mum. You know the routes I'm on. I don't hanker after the Mediterranean like some of the girls. I like the friendliness of the smaller airports and I enjoy being with the same crew and getting to know them. It's like being in a family.'

'I suppose I must get used to you not coming home so much these days.'

'It's the summer season. Peak time for charter flights abroad, plus lots of people wanting to holiday in British resorts.'

'Sounds like you've become a proper career girl, our Cora.' It was impossible not to notice the disappointment in her mother's voice.

'Tell you what, Mum. Why don't you take the train to Bristol next Wednesday and we'll spend a few hours together?

I'm not down to fly that day but if anything goes wrong, I'll phone you. OK?'

She rang off, feeling thoughtful. A career girl? That description didn't express how she saw herself, but was that how other people perceived her? People other than her mum and her ex-boyfriend?

* * *

Next day, after they landed at New-castle, she broached the subject with Tony. 'Am I becoming obsessed with my job?' They were strolling from the Dakota to the airline office.

'What's this all about?'

'Something my mother said. I think she's afraid I'll end up on the shelf.'

Tony roared with laughter. 'It must be difficult being female.'

'It's still a man's world, isn't it? We've come so far, but expectations to conform still haunt us.'

'You're not exactly in your dotage,'

he said. 'But to be fair, most parents worry about their offspring.' He pushed open the door for her. 'Let's sit down for a minute while it's quiet.'

She nodded. 'Over here?'

'Fine.' He dumped his briefcase on the floor. 'The trouble is, it's all or nothing with you, isn't it?'

'So you do think I'm obsessed with my job!'

'I think there's more to life than being good at your job,' said Tony. 'I enjoy spending time on the boat with you or seeing a film now and then. Helen knows you and I really are just good friends.'

'Sure. So does Ross, but only because I made sure he did. What's it got to do with him?'

Tony mimicked playing a violin. 'Here we go again. You're asking me to comment on your lifestyle but you totally ignore what I've already said. Right?'

'Um, yes, I suppose so.'

'Apart from being crewed together,

have you two ever spent time alone together?'

'Not since Reims.'

'What are you afraid of? Surely you don't think Ross will try and trap you into settling down? I'm enjoying getting to know Helen properly but it doesn't mean I'm buying her a ring. One day, who knows? Cut the poor fellow some slack, for goodness sake!'

'He and I are never crewed together these days. You know that.'

He smacked his forehead and turned to look at her. 'It wouldn't be too difficult for Ross and me to change places, with both skippers' approval of course. Or, if you asked Wendy to swap one of her days with you, I doubt it'd rock the schedules.'

She gasped. 'That would mean Ross and I would be crewed together and be free the next day.'

'If we could sort it, would that be so terrible?'

Cora thought hard. She missed Ross

so much these days. 'No,' she whispered. 'But he might run a mile.'

Tony groaned. 'Let's go and have a bite to eat and I'll try to convince you how he really feels, young lady.'

* * *

Next morning, Cora rushed into wakefulness, convinced she'd overslept, then relaxing back on the pillows as soon as she realised this was a day off. Tony's words drifted into her mind and she hugged herself, wondering whether she'd see Ross that evening. She'd been wrong, so very wrong, and she'd also been arrogant. Why should she imagine he wanted to marry her and dress her in a frilly pinafore? Tony and Helen kept in touch by phone and letter and met whenever it proved possible.

The idea of a similar relationship with Ross tempted her. Getting to know him, sharing information like birthdays and first memories, dissolving the awkwardness haunting the two of them, preventing them from going forward.

'This isn't a school playground,' Tony had said. 'I shan't tell Ross you'd like to go out with him. He feels he got off on the wrong foot with you and he still thinks you have a boyfriend, though he can't understand how you never seem to go out with the fellow.'

Cora had explained to Tony about writing to Dave, putting an end to a situation that never really was.

So, what had Tony said? 'Push a note under Ross's door tomorrow so he sees it when he gets back. Ask him to give you a knock and come in for a cup of tea.'

'I can't do that,' she'd said. 'He might stay out 'til all hours. I'd probably fall asleep in the chair while I waited for him.'

'But he hates clubs!' Tony had responded. 'OK. Leave a note asking him to ring you. Better still — let me ring him tomorrow and arrange to meet at the airport for a drink after his flight. I'll drive you there, Cora. When he comes into the bar, I'll shoot off and leave you two together.'

She'd laughed. Protested. Thanked him.

Cora spent the rest of the morning on chores, kept a hair appointment at three o'clock and was waiting on the pavement when Tony drew up at seven to collect her. He whistled as she got into the car. 'Anyone would think you'd dressed to impress,' he said.

'It's only because you're used to seeing me wearing uniform or those jeans I keep for the boat.'

'You look lovely in that yellow dress,' he said. 'Ross is a very lucky man.'

She shook her head and gazed straight ahead. 'I'd never have got in touch with him,' she said. 'I couldn't bear it if he'd changed his mind.'

'Believe me,' said Tony, 'he was over the moon when I explained my cunning plan.' He chatted about every subject under the sun except First Officer Anderson until he pulled into the airport car park.

'I hope Linda's not on duty,' said Cora. 'She's bound to wonder what we're doing here together.'

He tapped the side of his nose. 'Ah, but we've come to discuss my boat. I've decided to advertise it for renting so we're here to meet Ross because it's the only way the three of us can spend a couple of hours together.'

She nodded. 'Fair enough.'

'Let's go straight to the bar,' said Tony. 'We can see the DC3 touch down from there.'

★   ★   ★

But after they'd chatted with a customs officer they both knew and the man set off home, Tony checked his watch and frowned.

Cora's stomach lurched alarmingly. 'What is it?'

'The boys are late. I'll shoot downstairs and ask what's going on. You stay here.'

She nodded. 'Please don't be too

long. I've already got cold feet.'

He patted her hand. 'Don't be daft. How about another drink?'

'No thanks,' she said quickly. 'I'll read this magazine while you're gone.' She picked up an aviation periodical, knowing it wouldn't hold her attention but desperate not to keep staring out of the window, waiting for the aeroplane which so featured in her life these days.

Tony didn't take long. 'So much for my cunning plan,' he said. 'They're stuck at Liverpool. Mechanical problem. There's no chance of them flying back tonight. Another Dakota will come from Gatwick for us to fly tomorrow's schedule. That's aviation, I guess. All I can suggest is we go home and see what tomorrow brings.'

★ ★ ★

'I'm so sorry,' said Ross, taking the steps two at a time after Cora's passengers disembarked at Bristol next evening. 'We took the train back this morning.'

'You're apologising again,' said Cora. 'Was it you who broke my favourite aeroplane?'

He grinned. 'Not guilty, ma'am. Shall we try that quiet drink and chat now?'

'It's a lovely evening. What about a walk on the downs?'

'That's a much better idea.' He picked up her vanity case.

'Don't you want to see Tony?'

'No fear! It's you I want to see. I'll catch up with Cullen some other time.'

She felt relief and excitement wash over her as she stepped outside. But a tinge of shyness crept in. What if their time alone didn't live up to expectations?

Ross unlocked his dark green MG and placed their bags on the rear bench. Cora sank into the squishy leather bucket seat and waited for him to take his place beside her. The distinctive, throaty engine sound reminded her she'd never driven with him before.

'What a lovely car.'

'She's my pride and joy,' he said. 'But I want an even more beautiful lady in my life now, Cora. Do I really stand a chance?'

Her heart couldn't be swelling, surely? She felt shivery and thrilled and slightly frightened, all at the same time. It was a very different sentiment from the way she'd felt about Dave.

'It's all right,' said Ross. 'I don't intend rushing you. But I'd like us to spend as much time together as possible.'

'I'd like that too,' she said softly.

They drove in silence for a while.

'Shall we go home first?'

'That'd be good,' she said. 'I can change in two minutes flat.'

'Hotdog and a milkshake, then a walk?'

'Perfect.'

He reached out and squeezed her hand. 'I never thought this would actually happen,' he said. 'When Tony convinced me you wanted to see me as much as I wanted to see you, I could have jumped six feet in the air.' He changed gear, still holding her hand.

'I'd like to have seen that,' said Cora.

'When we fired up the Dakota yesterday evening and realised we had a problem, my first thought was you.'

'This won't work if I'm a distraction, Ross.'

'But don't you see?' Gently he released her hand. 'All this time we've been hoping to avoid one another, it's been niggling away at my emotions. And now we have the chance to see whether we can make a go of things, life will be much easier. For you as well as for me, I hope.'

She knew he spoke the truth. Now, could she be as honest with him as he'd been with her? *Come on, Cora.*

She took a deep breath. 'I felt devastated when Tony told me you'd been marooned in Liverpool. And this evening, when you came on board to find me, I wanted to tell you how lovely it was to see you.'

'Thank you,' he said. 'That's all I need to hear.'

'Oh no, it's not,' said Cora. 'You need to know my former boyfriend has been just that for many months now.'

Ross was frowning when she glanced at him. 'I jumped to conclusions,' he said. 'I've been stupid.'

Cora touched her forefinger to his lips. 'Don't you dare say you're sorry!'

They drove down Laurel Road, giggling like schoolchildren. Ross parked neatly, jumped out and ran round the vehicle to open her door. They stood on the pavement outside the Jelly residence, staring at one another as if unsure what came next.

Cora stood on tiptoe and lightly kissed Ross's mouth. He took her in his arms and kissed her back. When she opened her eyes again, he was gazing tenderly down at her.

'Jeans and jumpers,' he said.

'Downstairs in five minutes.' She

darted up the path ahead of him. So much for good resolutions. When the front room curtain in the landlord's flat twitched, she hastily unlocked the front door, hoping Ross hadn't noticed the interest shown by Mr and Mrs Jelly in their flying tenants.

16

'So how did it go?' Tony Cullen appeared beside Cora as she scooped up a handful of sweets for her tray.

'Nosy parker,' teased Cora, passing him a raspberry one. 'You be careful I don't cut your biscuit ration.'

He pretended to shudder. 'Perish the thought. You and Ross wasted no time scurrying off the night before last. Are you going to keep me in suspense?'

'I wouldn't dream of it,' she said. 'Not when you've been playing Cupid.'

'Ha! It was about time someone banged your heads together. Sounds as if you've at least reached an understanding, then?'

'I'll tell you later. If it's sunny in Newcastle, do you fancy a picnic? There must be a park?'

Tony set off up the cabin. 'Yep. A picnic sounds good. It'll leave us time for some cartoons too.'

She shook her head in amusement. The pilots' fondness for sugary biscuits and Snagglepuss adventures never failed to amaze her. She said as much to Tony when they reached the park at lunchtime.

'Teasing you about being Biscuit Monitress is fun,' he said. 'Watching Wile E. Coyote and the Road Runner is soothing too.'

'The boat's all about relaxing, isn't it? Even though you've put lots of hard work into it.'

'You've helped a lot, as has Ross of course, even if he didn't want to live aboard *High Flyer*. Funny how it's worked out that you each have a bedsit in the same house.'

'Just because Ross and I have become closer, doesn't mean I don't value spending time with you. It's one of the things we discussed the other night.' She offered him another sausage roll.

'Thanks,' said Tony. 'I did wonder if he might resent his best friend spending more time with his girlfriend than he can.'

Cora pierced her orange juice carton. 'It's no different for me, knowing he's lunching with Wendy, or sitting beside her, watching the same news shows as we do.'

'Well, there's the airport party to look forward to. I'm hoping Helen can come. Maybe the four of us can sit at the same table.'

'I'd forgotten about the party. If Helen comes she's welcome to sleep on my settee.'

'Thanks. That'd be great.' He bit into a cheese roll.

'A Castle Airways table sounds fun, and don't forget Wendy,' said Cora. 'She's going out with one of our regular passengers now.'

'I'm not surprised. Air hostesses make good wives, so they say.'

Cora screwed up a paper bag and threw it at him. 'Whereas pilots make dreadful husbands.'

'Definitely. They turn up late for

meals with excuses about fog down the route. They fall asleep at dinner parties and have to leave home to clock in for their flights, while all sensible folk are still sleeping.'

Cora smiled. 'You know I'm not ready for marriage, Tony. Ross is well aware of that too.'

Tony began gathering up the picnic things. 'So your chat was pretty comprehensive then?'

She rose and brushed crumbs from her skirt. 'Oh, yes. Ross and I are very fond of one another but we're not rushing into anything.'

'How fond, exactly?'

She burst out laughing. 'You're incorrigible, First Officer Cullen. OK, I'm in love with your friend and I think he feels the same about me.'

'You know Ross loves you, Air Hostess Murray, and I'm delighted for you both. Now let's go and find Bing. He said he'd see us outside the news cinema. There's time to see the show before we go back.'

With so much on her mind, Cora hadn't given any thought to the airport party to which everyone looked forward. One glance at her roster confirmed she'd be flying that day, whizzing across to Amsterdam, back to Bristol then leaving for the Isle of Man and back. She'd land, then hurry inside to change into her party dress.

Next time she arrived for duty, Cora found Linda at the check in desk. 'I'll be the one turning up with limp hair and a creased frock,' she said, looking over Linda's shoulder at the passenger manifest.

'Don't be silly,' said her friend. 'Bring in your dress that morning and I'll hang it somewhere safe. You can borrow my heated rollers after you land if you like. Although,' she added slyly, 'I doubt First Officer Anderson will criticise your appearance.'

Cora felt her cheeks warming. 'News travels fast around here,' she said.

'We all think it's lovely,' said Linda. 'Anyway, what are you wearing to the party? Long or short?'

'Short. I bought something a while back and this is the perfect opportunity to wear it. I don't get to many parties these days.'

'Join the club,' said Linda. 'Have a good day,' she called as her phone rang.

★ ★ ★

Cora and Ross took advantage of longer daylight hours so when she was on duty he drove to the airport to meet her. Sometimes they had a drink with Bing and Tony but mostly they went back to the house so Cora could change before they went walking, hand in hand on the downs.

On one occasion, she asked permission to swap days with Wendy so she could travel to Gatwick with Ross. It seemed odd to walk through the door of the Beehive again. Ross kissed her cheek and set off for a routine medical while Cora headed for the hostess headquarters, peering through glass panels 'til she found who she was looking for.

She knocked and poked her head around the door. 'Good morning, Jeanne.'

'Goodness, Cora, how lovely to see you.' Jeanne rose. 'Let me give you a hug — as long as my bump doesn't get in the way!'

'That's a pretty maternity dress,' said Cora.

Jeanne chuckled. 'My uniform's long gone. Castle, especially Maggie, have been kind to me, but my job here finishes on Friday. Then it's domesticity and motherhood for me!'

'You look delighted about it,' said Cora.

'I am. Are you here to see Maggie? She hasn't said anything.'

'No,' said Cora quickly. 'First Officer Anderson offered me a ride. He's due his medical today.'

'I see.' Jeanne's face split into a grin.

'That would explain why you and Wendy Baker changed duty days, but I guess your face says it all.'

'If only I didn't blush,' said Cora. 'OK. Ross and I are seeing each other as often as we can.'

Jeanne glanced at the board on the wall behind her desk. 'I imagine that's difficult, given you're not usually crewed together?'

'We have bedsits in the same house.'

Jeanne raised her eyebrows. 'Forgive me, but is that wise?'

Cora felt her cheeks turn even hotter. 'We're determined not to let our relationship interfere with our jobs. I wouldn't dream of living with him.'

'Not ever?' Jeanne teased, easing herself back into her chair.

'I'm not looking too far into the future at the moment.'

'Very wise. Now, Cora, you can't leave without calling on Maggie.'

'Oh dear.' Cora bit her lip.

Jeanne picked up the phone. 'I'll tell her you're here. Her office is the next one along. I'm on my lunch break at 12.00 so if you fancy joining me, you know where I'll be.'

Cora knocked but didn't enter Maggie's sanctum until she heard the chief air hostess respond. 'This is a surprise, Cora. Do sit down.'

'Thank you, Miss Martin. I had the chance of a lift to Gatwick so I thought I'd try and see a few people.'

Maggie's lips twitched. 'I did hear First Officer Anderson was booked for his medical today. So, have you something to tell me?'

'No, nothing to tell you, Miss Martin.' Cora watched Maggie drop her gaze to Cora's hands, as if checking for an engagement ring.

'I hear nothing but good things about you,' said Maggie.

Cora gulped. 'I love my job.'

'It shows. Now, I shall put this in writing of course, but I can tell you we'd like you to continue working for us after the summer schedules end, Cora.'

Cora almost jumped from her seat. 'That's brilliant news. Thank you very much.'

Maggie nodded. 'How would you feel about a transfer?'

'Me? Do you mean to Gatwick?'

'Mainly on the Elizabethan as a number two hostess over the winter, then we'd evaluate you next spring.'

'But who'd want to leave Gatwick to take my place?' Cora's pulse had ratcheted up a notch or six.

'I've received a request from another hostess for a Bristol transfer. I can't reveal her name but she'd be ideal.'

'But I'm happy where I am, Miss Martin. I can think of at least two girls flying the West Country routes who'd love to be based here.'

'Are you taking over my job, Air Hostess Murray?' In a twinkling, Maggie's expression became glacial.

'I'm sorry. You caught me by surprise.'

'I had no idea you'd walk in here today, but I'm glad you did. Maybe you need to talk things over with . . . your family?'

'No.' Cora shook her head. 'My parents are used to me living away from home. It's, well, it's a bit embarrassing.'

Maggie leaned her elbows on her desk and propped up her chin. 'Because you're in love?'

'We're not engaged or anything.'

Maggie sighed. 'I watched your faces that very first day Ross bumped into you in the corridor. So I'm not surprised about this development. But you must realise Castle can't run its schedules based on the romantic preferences of its pilots and cabin crew?'

'Of course. I'm just surprised you want to move me to Gatwick.'

'While your boyfriend remains at Bristol? That's aviation, Cora. How would you feel if, a couple of months down the line, Ross was whisked back to Gatwick, or sent to Glasgow, leaving you in Bristol?'

'I'd have to take it on the chin, wouldn't I?'

'That's better. This is promotion, Cora. Believe me, Ross won't turn down promotion when it's his turn to move to a bigger aeroplane.'

Cora nodded. 'I wouldn't expect him to.'

'Good girl. Now, Jeanne's just passed my door so go and chat with her. That doesn't mean I'm suggesting you follow in her footsteps and marry in secret! But I'm sure she has plenty of advice on juggling romance and career.'

★ ★ ★

'Believe me, I had no idea Maggie would spring a transfer on me.'

Ross unlocked the MG. 'You must be pleased. It proves she thinks a lot of you.'

'She petrified me at first,' said Cora, hopping in. 'Still does! But it's amazing to think she wants me at Gatwick.'

Cora asked how Ross's medical had gone but couldn't resist returning to her news. 'Fliss came into the cafeteria so she brought her tray over and sat with us. We had a lovely gossip. I know I shouldn't have said anything but I couldn't resist telling her. Jeanne knew anyway, of course. And guess what — Fliss has been made permanent too. She wonders whether we could share a flat together. Wouldn't that be great?' She glanced sideways. 'Ross?'

'Oh, I'm over the moon. Don't mind me.'

'Look, I'm sorry if I'm boring you.'

He puffed air through his lips. 'It's not that! I'm sorry I can't be more enthusiastic. Oh, here we go again, apologising! But we haven't even met each other's family yet and before we know it, you'll be packing up and leaving.'

Her heart did the customary flip-flop, signalling she couldn't bear the thought of parting from him. How could she have been so insensitive? 'I'm so sorry, darling.'

'I can't drive on like this. We have to stop and talk it through.' They travelled in silence until Ross indicated left and pulled into a tree-lined side street. Beneath a lime tree, its foliage a bright green cloud, he cut the engine. 'That's the first time you've called me darling.'

'Really? I hadn't thought about it.'

'I had. It means a great deal. You're not the kind of girl to say the word lightly. I've learned that much about you.' He took her hand and pressed it to his lips. 'I know you have to move on. Who knows where the airline will send me next, anyway? But I think we should consider putting things on a more formal basis.'

17

She frowned. 'I'm not sure what you mean.'

'I want us to become engaged, Cora. If you're wearing my ring, I'll be a whole lot happier. You're going to be flying with different crews, meeting lots of new people — surely I don't need to spell it out?'

'The fact that you don't trust me?'

'That's not true and you know it. I spend a lot of time with your chum, Wendy. You spend even more time with Tony, because of the boat.'

'Well, then?'

'Surely you agree that if we become engaged, everyone will know we belong to one another?'

She stared straight ahead. 'It's far too early for that kind of commitment.'

'Oh, fine. If that's how you feel, I'm sorry I asked.' His knuckles gleamed white as his hands gripped the steering wheel.

'Please don't let's have a row. Please don't drive on while you're angry.'

He sighed, then turned and reached out his hand to stroke her hair. 'I love you, Cora.'

She snuggled against him. 'And I love you, Ross. But, can't we wait a little bit longer?'

'Because I got engaged to Nicole in a hurry? Is that what's worrying you?'

She didn't answer.

'OK. Point taken. I'm a different person now but I can't expect you to know that.' He managed a shaky smile.

Cora pulled away from him and turned her head to hide her welling tears.

'Look at me, sweetheart. Please.'

She shook her head.

'Oh, Cora.' He took her in his arms and she clung to him.

'I love you so much, Ross, but I need to take this next step. Prove to myself and to you and my parents — yes, and to Maggie Martin — that I can handle a challenge.'

He brushed her teardrops away with his two thumbs very gently. 'Who am I to trample on your dreams? I shan't stop loving you, even though you're just as darned stubborn as I am about my flying.'

She leaned closer and kissed him on the mouth.

He groaned. 'We'd better get on our way, you temptress. I have a favourite tearoom down the route. I'll buy you cold lemonade and chocolate éclairs on the terrace. How's that for an idea?'

* * *

Ross insisted on getting up early on his day off to drive Cora and her suitcase to the airport on the day of the party. 'I'm afraid I'll have to charge you excess baggage,' he joked, heaving her case into his boot.

'It's OK for you.' She smiled. 'You

can turn up tonight looking well-groomed. By the time I've served four plane-loads of passengers, I shall look like a damp tea-towel.'

'Don't fish for compliments'.

Cora felt nothing but relief that Ross wasn't pestering her about becoming engaged. She knew she wanted to spend the rest of her life with him but she also realised the importance of getting the travel bug out of her system. To do so, she must rein in her emotions as firmly as she fixed passengers' seatbelts.

Ross wandered over to the Dakota for a chat with Tony while Cora made her preparations. He gave her a quick kiss on the cheek and clattered down the steps as Linda appeared in the distance, leading her flock.

Cora faced a day of take-offs and landings, full complements of passengers and what turned out to be her best bar takings ever. Bing and Tony achieved smooth-as-satin landings and Cora felt a thrill of anticipation as they flew across the Bristol Channel towards home. The crew call buzzer sounded as she stowed away clean cups and tiffin trays, sending her up the aisle, purposefully but calmly.

Bing turned round as she appeared at his right shoulder. Tony was focusing upon the numerous dials and switches. 'Cora,' said the skipper, 'we've had to feather one engine. This means I've advised the tower we'll be making an emergency landing. When you return to the cabin, I'll make an announcement to the passengers and when it's time to fasten seatbelts, you must ensure everyone is in the correct position. You know the drill.'

Her stomach lurched. Yes, she knew the drill: removing shoes, sharp objects from pockets, spectacles, even false teeth. No problem. But the implication was enormous.

Cora confirmed her understanding and left. She felt strangely calm, knowing her training would see her through. Ten passengers remained on board. Smiling serenely, she headed back to her galley and made sure everything was secured.

Captain Crosby's deep, calm voice grabbed the passengers' attention. Cora stood still, waiting to note any signs of acute distress. As soon as the seatbelt sign flashed on, she began making her checks, then advised Bing that everyone was prepared.

'Are you OK?' Tony turned around.

'I'm fine. Remember we've a party to go to, First Officer.'

'That's my girl,' said Bing. 'It's a wee bit foggy but that's the least of our problems.'

A shiver ran down Cora's spine. She wondered if Ross had heard about their predicament. Was he pacing the office? Or, oblivious, was he chatting with someone in the bar? She let herself out, knowing each passenger waited to see her expression. She nodded to every single one of them before taking an aisle seat across from a woman travelling alone, allowing sight of all her flock.

303

Cora found it unnerving being unable to spot the usual landmarks on descent. She didn't feel quite so brave now that Bing's wee bit of fog had turned into swirling mist swathing the windows, and Pappa, snagged by turbulence, buffeted and rocked like a dog tugging on its lead. *Please let us land safely!* Cora's unspoken prayer was doubtless repeated in everyone's head.

Down . . . down . . . surely they must land any moment? Seconds later, Cora's mouth dried as the skipper's voice came over the PA system, giving a terse order to adopt the bracing position.

Feet planted securely on the floor, straining forward, hands supporting her head, Cora knew no one could ask for a better crew than Bing and Tony. The Dakota's wheels touched down but no one relaxed. She sensed a tussle between man and metal as the pilot strained to maintain stability and bring his precious cargo home.

After they taxied to a halt, a little

cheer went up. The man nearest Cora turned around and grinned. 'That landing was a greaser. The captain deserves a pint!'

Cora snapped open her seatbelt and rose. 'He might just get one,' she said.

One by one, the passengers disembarked. There was no sign of Bing and Tony. Cora was about to hurry up the slope to congratulate them when a tall figure loomed in the doorway.

She caught a whiff of lemon aftershave, then Ross's arms were around her and he was hugging her as if he'd never, ever let her go. 'Thank God,' he said. 'Oh, my darling girl, are you all right? I've been so, so afraid.'

'I'm fine,' she said when he loosened his hold, allowing her to breathe again. 'But this has made me realise how much I love you, Ross. How precious what we have is.'

He nodded. 'Let's see how the boys are, shall we?'

His voice had been husky. Blinking away tears of relief, Cora led the way to the cockpit. Inside, Bing and Tony sat chatting as if waiting for her to bring another lot of coffee and biscuits.

Ross leaned over to speak to them. 'What a landing, Skipper,' he said. 'Not that I should be surprised with you at the controls.'

'All down to my first officer,' said Bing. 'Couldn't have done it better myself.'

18

It felt unreal, changing into a red frock and sparkling party shoes. Cora dabbed on some of her favourite Mitsouko and pulled out the heated rollers Linda had placed in her hair.

'You look wonderful,' said Wendy, walking in.

'You look pretty good yourself,' said Cora. 'I told you that misty green was your colour.'

'We only just got here. Ross told us about your emergency landing.' She hugged Cora. 'Weren't you frightened?'

'A bit. I don't want to sound like Perfect Petunia, but Maggie was right. Training does get you through. Not to mention having an amazing captain and first officer. Is my hair OK at the back?'

Wendy chuckled. 'It's lovely. You're a real pro, Air Hostess Murray. I'm going to miss you.'

'What do you mean?' Cora put down her hairbrush, wondering how Wendy could possibly know about her transfer to Gatwick.

'Please don't say anything yet, but Richard and I are getting married.'

'The passenger you told me about? Goodness, that's quick.'

'He's being posted up north and he proposed to me last weekend. I'm so happy, Cora. I'm not as dedicated to this job as you are. I'm writing to Maggie tomorrow, giving her my notice, but I'll see the season out of course.'

Cora's thoughts whirled. When Wendy left, Maggie would need to fill her position too. The chief hostess had only mentioned one person wanting a Bristol transfer. Would Maggie decide to ask Cora to stay on now? But it was no good. Decisions had been made. She must hold her tongue.

'Come and meet Richard,' said Wendy. 'And you must be longing to see Ross.'

The whole of the concourse was given over to the party. Tables and chairs were grouped around a space for dancing and a small band had launched into a medley of pop hits. When they followed 'Shakin' All Over' with 'Nowhere to Run', Cora decided someone had a black sense of humour and looked around for Tony.

A pleasant-looking young man with sandy hair and an impish grin claimed Wendy, who looked as though she'd got all she ever wanted in the world. Ross appeared beside Cora and put his arm around her waist. Helen came forward too.

'Where are my boys?' Cora turned to Helen. 'It's lovely to see you again.'

'You too. Bing and Tony have been speaking to ops. The chief pilot wanted a de-briefing.'

'I hope he realises just how amazing they were tonight,' Cora said sternly.

'There speaks the Biscuit Monitress,' said a voice.

She whirled around to find Tony

grinning at her. He took his place beside Helen and suddenly Bing was there too, his arm around a sweet-faced woman dressed in a long, dark green dress.

'Meet Mrs Bing,' said Captain Crosby.

Everyone was laughing, chatting and ordering drinks but Ross didn't let Cora out of his sight. As the band stopped playing a Beatles' number and launched into 'Back In My Arms Again', Cora's golden-haired first officer led her on to the dance floor. She nestled against his shoulder as they moved in harmony. 'We need to talk,' she said after a moment.

'I agree,' said Ross. 'You first.'

'No, you first.'

'OK,' they said simultaneously.

'Whoops, sorry,' he said.

'My fault,' said Cora.

Ross took a deep breath. 'Tonight, when I heard you were coming in on one engine, my heart almost stopped. I realised just how much I loved you. I think, I mean I hope, you feel the same.' He gazed down at her. 'Say you'll marry me, Cora? I don't mean like tomorrow or even next week. But, when you feel ready. In the meantime, wherever you're based, please say you'll wear my ring!'

'Yes. Yes, please. It's what I want too, Ross. Ouch, that was my toe!'

'I'm sorry, darling. I thought you'd be sure to say no.'

'I shan't apologise for changing my mind!' She laughed up at him.

'I love you so much, Biscuit Monitress,' he said, stroking her cheek.

'Not as much as I love you, Pirate,' she said.

They were dancing on the same spot when the band moved on to play 'I Do'. They didn't even notice when Tony, Helen, Richard, Wendy, Bing and Mrs Bing gathered round and applauded.

THE END

We do hope that you have enjoyed reading this large print book.

Did you know that all of our titles are available for purchase?

We publish a wide range of high quality large print books including:
**Romances, Mysteries, Classics
General Fiction
Non Fiction and Westerns**

Special interest titles available in large print are:
**The Little Oxford Dictionary
Music Book, Song Book
Hymn Book, Service Book**

Also available from us courtesy of Oxford University Press:
**Young Readers' Dictionary
(large print edition)
Young Readers' Thesaurus
(large print edition)**

For further information or a free brochure, please contact us at:
**Ulverscroft Large Print Books Ltd.,
The Green, Bradgate Road, Anstey,
Leicester, LE7 7FU, England.
Tel:** (00 44) 0116 236 4325
Fax: (00 44) 0116 234 0205

Other titles in the
Linford Romance Library:

ANNA'S RETURN

Sally Quilford

Anna Silverton and Janek Dabrowski escape war-torn Europe together, forging a friendship that carries them through difficult times. Even when they are apart, Anna dreams of Janek coming for her so they can be a family. Then, when she is accused of harming her half-brother, Teddy, she runs away, finding Janek again. Their childhood friendship soon turns to a tentative love, but the vicious lies told about Anna force them to part once again. Can the couple ever have a future together?

THE CAPTAIN'S WIFE

Jean Robinson

1975. After years struggling to cope with a childless marriage and the loneliness of being left behind while her seafaring husband Max is away, Sarah finally persuades him to take her with him on a four-month voyage. But she is not prepared for the change in him once in command of his ship, and often feels resentful that he has so little time for her. Over the months she and Geoffrey, the chief officer, are drawn together for comfort, and perhaps more — but is that what Sarah really wants?